The Mystery of the Invisible Dog

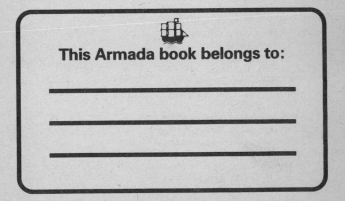

This Armada book belongs to:

_____

_____

_____

The Three Investigators in

The Mystery of the Invisible Dog

Text by M. V. Carey
Based on characters created by Robert Arthur

ARMADA

First published in the U.K. in 1976 by
William Collins Sons & Co. Ltd., London and Glasgow
First published in Armada in 1979
This impression 1988

Armada is an imprint of
the Children's Division, part of
the Collins Publishing Group,
8 Grafton Street, London W1X 3LA

Printed and bound in Great Britain by
William Collins Sons & Co. Ltd, Glasgow

Contents

A Word
from Alfred Hitchcock

Greetings, mystery fans!

Again it is my pleasure to introduce that trio of young detectives known as the Three Investigators. They specialize in unusual cases, bizarre happenings, and eerie events. And unusual, bizarre, and eerie their new adventure certainly is! In it, they encounter one haunted man, a phantom priest, a would-be mystic with the ability to walk through walls, and also the image of a demon dog—a very solid image which manages to be completely invisible.

For any reader who is meeting the Three Investigators for the first time, I shall duly state that Jupiter Jones, the leader of the group, is a plump young lad with a keen mind and insatiable curiosity. Pete Crenshaw is quick and athletic, and Bob Andrews, a bookish fellow, keeps the records for the group and has a decided talent for research. All three reside in the coastal town of Rocky Beach, California, on the outskirts of Los Angeles.

So much for introductions. You may now turn to Chapter One and commence reading!

ALFRED HITCHCOCK

I

The Haunted Man

IT WAS TWILIGHT—the abrupt, chill twilight of
late December—when Jupiter Jones, Pete Crenshaw, and Bob Andrews first came to Paseo Place.
They walked up the street past a park where a
few late roses still bloomed in spite of the cold.
Next to the park was a stucco house with a sign
announcing that this was St Jude's Rectory.
Beyond the rectory, lights glowed behind the
stained-glass windows of a little church and an
organ boomed and droned. The boys could hear
children's voices piping phrases from an old
hymn.

They passed the church and came to an apartment house which look d very private. On the
street level it had a row of garages. Above these
were two storeys of apartments. All of the
windows had carefully closed curtains, as if the
tenants wanted to shut out the world.

"This is it," said Jupiter Jones. "Number 402
Paseo Place, and it is now exactly half past five.
We're right on time."

To the right of the garages, broad flagstone
steps led up one flight towards a gate. A man in a
camel-coloured jacket was coming down them

now. He passed the boys without looking at them.

Jupe started up the steps, with Pete and Bob close behind him. Suddenly Pete jumped and let out a startled exclamation.

Jupe stopped. Out of the corner of his eye he saw a small, dark shape glide away down the stairs.

"It's only a cat," said Bob.

"I almost stepped on it." Pete shivered and pulled his dark ski jacket closer around him. "A black cat!"

Bob laughed. "Come on! You don't really believe they're bad luck!"

Jupe reached for the latch on the gate. Beyond, in the centre of a flagstoned courtyard, was a large swimming pool surrounded by chairs and tables. As Jupe opened the gate, floodlights went on in the pool and in the shrubbery that rimmed the court.

"No peddlers allowed!" said a nasal, raspy voice almost at Jupe's elbow.

A door next to the gate had opened. In the doorway stood a thick-bodied, red-haired woman who squinted at the boys through rimless glasses.

"I don't care whether you're selling magazine subscriptions or candy or taking up a collection to help orphaned canaries," said the woman. "I don't want my tenants disturbed."

"Mrs Bortz!"

The woman looked up and past the boys. A thin, silver-haired man had come down a stairway from a balcony that overlooked the courtyard.

"I believe these are the young gentlemen I am expecting," said the man.

"I am Jupiter Jones." Jupe made the statement in the precise, formal way that was characteristic of him. He stepped aside and nodded towards his friends. "Pete Crenshaw and Bob Andrews. I assume that you are Mr Fenton Prentice."

"I am," said the elderly man. He glanced at the woman in the doorway. "We do not need you, Mrs Bortz," he added.

"Well!" exclaimed the woman. She retreated into her apartment and slammed her door.

"Nosy old crone," said Fenton Prentice. "Please ignore her. Most of the other people who live in this building are reasonably civilized. Won't you come with me?"

The boys followed Mr Prentice up the stairs to the balcony. Only a few feet from the top of the stairs was a door which Fenton Prentice unlocked. He ushered the boys into a room with a beamed ceiling and a chandelier which appeared to be very old and precious. On one table stood a small artificial Christmas tree, decorated with exquisite little ornaments.

"Please sit down." Mr Prentice waved vaguely toward some chairs, then locked his door behind him.

"It was good of you to come so quickly," he said. "I was afraid that, this being Christmas week, you might have made other plans."

"As it happens, we find ourselves with a little free time," said Jupiter graciously. "We have few commitments before school resumes next week."

Pete choked back a laugh. The three boys had no plans at all for the rest of the holidays, other than avoiding Jupe's Aunt Mathilda. She had plenty of plans. All of them involved putting the boys to work!

"And now," Jupiter went on grandly, "if you will kindly tell us why you summoned us, we will determine whether or not we can be of assistance."

"Whether or not!" echoed Mr Prentice. "But you *must* help me. I need action immediately!" His voice shook suddenly and went up in pitch. "I cannot put up with what has been happening here!"

He paused a moment to calm himself, and continued, "You *are* the Three Investigators, are you not? This *is* your card?" He removed a business card from his wallet and showed it to the boys.

THE THREE INVESTIGATORS

"We Investigate Anything"

?   ?   ?

First Investigator – JUPITER JONES
Second Investigator – PETER CRENSHAW
Records and Research – BOB ANDREWS

Jupe glanced at the card and nodded in recognition.

"The friend who gave me this card," said Mr

Prentice, "told me that you boys are detectives with a great interest in things which are . . . well, rather unusual."

"That is true," said Jupe. "The question marks on our card, symbolizing the unknown, might be taken as a statement of that interest. In the past, we have succeeded in solving some rather bizarre puzzles. But until you tell us what is troubling you, we won't know if we can possibly help. We are prepared to try, of course. In fact, we have already begun preliminary work on your case. After we received your letter this morning, we investigated you!"

"What?" cried Prentice. "What impertinence!"

"If you are to be our client, don't you think we should know something about you?" demanded Jupe reasonably.

"I am a very private person," said Prentice. "I don't care to have anyone prying into my affairs."

"No one can be totally private," said Jupiter Jones, "and Bob is a first-rate researcher. Bob, would you tell Mr Prentice what you discovered?"

Bob grinned. He admired Jupe's ability to get the upper hand in most situations. He took a small note pad out of his pocket and opened it. "You were born in Los Angeles, Mr Prentice," he said. "You are now in your seventies. Your father, Giles Prentice, made a fortune in real estate. You inherited that fortune. You arc not married. You travel often and you give generously to museums and to individual artists. The newspapers refer to you as a patron of the arts."

"I seldom bother with newspapers," said Mr Prentice.

"But they bother about you," Jupe remarked. "You do seem to take a great interest in the arts," he added, looking around the room.

The living room was actually a luxurious showcase for an art collection. Paintings hung on the walls, porcelain figures stood on low tables, and here and there were lamps which might have come from some Moorish palace.

"Very well," said Prentice. "There isn't anything wrong with taking an interest in beautiful things. But that has nothing to do with what's going on here."

"What *is* going on here?" asked Jupiter.

Prentice glanced over his shoulder, as if he feared someone might be listening in the next room. When he spoke, his voice was almost a whisper. "I am being haunted," he said.

The Three Investigators stared at him.

"You don't believe me," said Prentice. "I was afraid you wouldn't, but it's true. Someone gets in here when I'm away. I come back and find that my things aren't the way I left them. Once I found my desk drawer partly open. Someone had been reading my letters."

"This is a large apartment house," Jupiter pointed out. "Is there a manager? Would the manager have a master key?"

Prentice sniffed. "That loathsome Bortz woman is the manager, but she does not have a key to this apartment. I had a special lock installed. And if you are going to ask about servants, I don't have any. And don't even suggest that someone comes in through the windows. I don't have any windows opening on to the balcony. The windows in this room look out on to the street and they're twenty feet above the sidewalk. In the bedroom and the den, the windows overlook the church and they're also many feet above the ground. No one could possibly get in through the windows without a long ladder, and that would most certainly be noticed."

"There *must* be a second key," said Pete. "Someone uses it when you're not here and—"

Fenton Prentice held up his hand. "No. Oh, someone comes when I'm gone, but that's not the worst of it." Again he looked around as if afraid that he was not alone with the boys. "Sometimes he comes when I'm here. I've . . . I've seen him. He comes and he goes, and no door needs to open."

"What does he look like?" asked Jupiter.

Mr Prentice rubbed his hands together nervously. "That's the sort of question a policeman would ask," he said. "But he wouldn't believe my answer. That's why I called you instead of the police. What I see is . . . not quite a person. It's more like a shadow. Sometimes I'm reading and I can feel it. I feel that there is a presence here. If I look up, I may see it. Once I saw someone in the hall—someone tall and thin. I started to speak. Perhaps I shouted. He didn't turn, but went into the den. I went after him. The room was empty."

"May I look at the den?" asked Jupiter.

"Certainly." Prentice went to a small, square hall that opened off the living room. Jupe followed him through it into a large, dimly lit room which had shelves of books, deep leather chairs, and a big antique desk. The windows here were on the side of the building. Through the open curtains Jupe could see the church next door. The organ no longer boomed and children's voices could be heard in the street; apparently choir practice was over.

"There is no way out of this room," said Prentice, "except for the door to the hall. Don't suggest a secret passage. I've lived in this apartment for many years, and I know there are no secret passages."

"How long have you had this feeling that you are being invaded by some . . . some presence?" asked Jupiter.

"For several months," Prentice answered. "I . . . I didn't want to believe it at first. I thought I was imagining things because I was overtired. But it's happened so often that now I'm sure I'm not imagining things."

Jupe saw that the man wanted very badly to be believed. "I suppose anything is possible," said the First Investigator.

"Then you will take my case?" said Prentice. "You will investigate?"

"I'll have to discuss it with my friends," said Jupe. "May we call you in the morning?"

Prentice nodded and left the room. Jupe hesitated, wondering. Suddenly something stirred in the shadowy corner near the bookshelves.

Jupe stared. "Pete!" he said.

"You call me?" answered Pete. His voice was loud and hearty and it came from the living room.

"Pete!" Jupe shouted, and lunged to turn on the overhead light.

A second later the room was brightly lighted and Pete was in the doorway. "What's the matter?" he asked.

"You . . . you were in the living room when I called," said Jupiter Jones.

"Yes. What is it? You look like you've seen a ghost."

"I thought I saw you," said Jupiter Jones. "Over in the corner. I thought you were standing there."

Jupe shook himself. "Must have been a shadow," he said. He brushed past Pete and went into the living room. "We'll be in touch with you to-morrow," he promised Mr Prentice.

"Very well." The man who believed he was being haunted unlocked the door and stood aside to let the boys out.

Then they heard a sound that might have been a backfire—or a shot.

Pete almost leaped through the door. He looked down over the balcony railing. The courtyard below was empty, but behind the house, someone was shouting. A gate slammed and footsteps pounded on some staircase that the boys couldn't see. Then, from a passage which led into the rear of the court, a running figure came into view. A man wearing a dark windbreaker and with a black ski hood pulled over his head raced past the pool and out through the front gate to the street.

Pete dashed for the stairs. He was almost at the bottom when a policeman appeared at the back of the courtyard.

"Okay, buddy!" shouted the cop. "Hold it right there or I'll let you have it!"

A second policeman came pelting into the court. Pete saw that both men had drawn their guns. He froze where he was on the stairway and raised his hands in the air!

2

The Search in the Night

"MIKE," said the younger of the two policemen, "I don't think he's the guy."

"Dark windbreaker, light-coloured trousers," said the other policeman. "He could have tossed that ski mask somewhere."

"The man with the ski mask ran through here and out the front gate," said Pete quickly. "I saw him."

Jupe and Bob came down the stairs with Mr Prentice.

"This young man has been with me for the last half hour," said Prentice to the policeman.

Sirens screamed as patrol cars converged on the area.

"C'mon," said the younger officer. "We're wasting time."

The two policemen hurried out through the front gate, just as the door to Mrs Bortz's apartment opened.

"Mr Prentice, what have these boys been up to?" demanded Mrs Bortz.

On the right side of the court, a door opened and a young man stumbled out. He was rubbing his eyes, as if just awakened. Jupe looked at him and started slightly.

"What is it?" whispered Bob.

"Nothing," said Jupe. "I'll tell you later."

"Mr Prentice, you did not answer me!" snapped Mrs Bortz. "What have these boys been up to?"

"It's no concern of yours," said Prentice. "The police are searching for someone—some felon, no doubt—who ran in from the back alley and then went out through the front gate."

"A burglar," said the young man who had come from the apartment beyond the pool. He was wearing a dark sweater and light tan trousers, and his bare feet had been shoved into sneakers. Jupe, who prided himself on his ability to notice details, saw that the young man's lank, dark hair hadn't been washed recently. He was hardly taller than Pete and was extremely thin.

"Sonny Elmquist, you're so clever!" said Mrs Bortz. "How do *you* know it's a burglar they're looking for?"

The young man named Sonny Elmquist swallowed nervously, and his Adam's apple bobbed above the top of his sweater. "What else could it be?" he asked.

"Spread out!" shouted someone on the street outside. "Check the alleys—and check out that church!"

The Three Investigators and Fenton Prentice went out and stood on the front steps of the apartment house. There were four patrol cars on the street. Flashlights swept back and forth as policemen poked into shrubbery and peered down driveways in search of the fugitive in the black ski mask. A helicopter clattered overhead, its beam probing alleys. In other doorways up and down the street stood more groups of onlookers.

"He couldn't have gone far!" shouted one searcher. "He's got to be around here somewhere."

A chunky man with thick grey hair stood at the kerb talking excitedly to a police lieutenant. As the boys watched, he turned, then hurried toward the apartment-house steps. "Fenton!" he called. "Fenton Prentice!"

Mr Prentice went down the steps, and the man took him by the arm and began to tell him something. Prentice listened intently. He seemed to have forgotten that the boys were there.

Pete nudged Jupe. "Let's go see what they're doing at the church," he suggested.

At the church, the doors stood open. A number of people, including Mrs Bortz and Sonny Elmquist, had gathered on the pavement to stare into the interior of the building. A pair of patrolmen were searching inside, bending to peer under pews.

Jupe went quietly through the crowd and up two steps into the church. He saw candles glimmering in racks in front of the altar—red and blue and green vigil lights. He saw motionless figures—statues on pedestals and statues on the floor, in corners and against the walls. He also saw a police sergeant confronting a stout, red-faced man who had a sheaf of booklets in his hands.

"I tell you, nobody came in here," said the stout

man. "I was here the whole time. I'd have seen if anybody came in."

"Sure, sure," said the sergeant. "Now if you don't mind, please leave. We have to search the building."

The sergeant looked around at Jupe. "You, too, kid," he said. "Out!"

Jupe retreated along with the irate man, who still clutched his booklets. Outside, a thin, rather young man dressed in black with a round white collar—obviously a priest—had joined the spectators. So had a short woman whose grey hair was twisted into a bun at the back of her neck.

"Father McGovern!" cried the man with the booklets. "You tell them. I was in the church the whole time. Whoever they're looking for, he couldn't have got in without my seeing him."

"Ah, now, Earl!" said the priest. "They must look, you know."

"What?" Earl put a hand up to his ear.

"They must look," the priest repeated in a louder tone. "Where were you just now?"

"In the choir loft, picking up the hymn booklets, like always," said Earl.

"Hah!" The grey-haired woman laughed. "A herd of elephants could stampede in there and you'd not hear them. Deaf as a post you are, and getting deafer every day."

Someone in the crowd chuckled.

"Now, Mrs O'Reilly," said the priest, gently chiding. "Come along. We'll go to the rectory and you'll make us a nice cup of tea, and when the police have finished, Earl can come back and lock up. It's not really our concern, you know "

The crowd parted to make way for Earl, the priest, and the woman. When they had disappeared into the stucco house next door, one of the onlookers grinned at the boys.

" You live around here?" asked the man, raising his voice to be heard above the circling helicopter.

"No," said Bob.

"Never a dull moment." The man nodded toward the rectory. "Earl's the caretaker, and he thinks he runs the parish. Mrs O'Reilly's the housekeeper in the rectory, and she thinks *she* runs the parish. Father McGovern's got his hands full keeping the two of them from running *him* right into the ground."

"More than a pastor should have to put up with," put in a woman. "An old-country Irishwoman who sees spooks in every corner and a stubborn janitor who thinks the church would fall down if he weren't there to hold it up."

The sergeant and the patrolmen emerged from the church. The sergeant scanned the crowd on the pavement. "Okay!" he called. "Where's the guy who's supposed to be in charge here?"

"He's having a cup of tea with the pastor," volunteered the man who had spoken to the Investigators. "I'll get him."

The police helicopter made one last pass above the neighbourhood, then disappeared towards the north.

The lieutenant who had been talking to Mr

Prentice's friend came down the street.

"Nothing in the church," reported the sergeant.

The lieutenant sighed. "Beats me how he got out of the neighbourhood so fast," he said. "The helicopter usually spots them, unless they've got a place to go to ground. Okay. We can't do anything more tonight."

Earl the caretaker bustled up from the parish house and stamped into the church, slamming the door behind him.

In a few minutes, the police cars had pulled away. The spectators drifted back to their homes.

Jupiter, Pete, and Bob walked back to the apartment house. Fenton Prentice was still there talking to the grey-haired man.

"Mr Prentice," said Jupiter, "I'm sorry to interrupt, but—"

"It's quite all right." Mr Prentice looked very weary. "I have just learned from Charles—from Mr Niedland here—what this furor is about."

"My brother's home was broken into," said Prentice's friend. "He had a house on Lucan Court. That's the next street over."

"I'm very sorry, Charles," said Mr Prentice. "This must be especially painful for you."

"For you, too," said Charles Niedland. "Don't let it upset you too much, Fenton, and try to get some rest. I'll talk to you in the morning."

Charles Niedland went in through the courtyard and out through the rear passageway which led, Jupe supposed, to an alley and to the buildings on the street behind Paseo Place. Fenton Prentice sat down on the steps as if he were too exhausted to stand any longer. "What a desecration!" he exclaimed.

"The burglary?" asked Bob.

"Edward Niedland was my friend," explained Prentice. "My friend, my protégé, and a very fine artist. He died two weeks ago, of pneumonia."

The boys were silent.

"A great loss," said Fenton Prentice. "Very hard for me to accept, and very hard for his brother Charles. And now to have his home broken into!"

"Was anything taken?" asked Bob.

"Charles doesn't know yet. He is going to check the contents of the house right now, with the police."

There were brisk steps on the pavement behind the boys. Bob and Pete turned. A hearty, robust-appearing man in a beige sweater strode jauntily to the flagstone stairs. At the sight of Prentice sitting there, and the boys hovering near him, the man stopped and stared.

"Anything the matter?" he asked.

"There has been a burglary in the neighbourhood, Mr Murphy," said Prentice. "The police have been searching."

"Oh," said the newcomer. "I thought there were a lot of squad cars around. Did they get the guy?"

"Unfortunately, they did not."

"Too bad," said Murphy. He went around Prentice and up the steps. A second later the boys heard an apartment door inside the courtyard open and close.

"I think I will retire upstairs," said Mr Prentice. He stood up weakly. "Please call me tomorrow with your agreement to help, boys. I can't go on this way much longer. First the haunting intruder, then Edward's death, and now the burglary—it's more than a man can bear!"

3

The Magic Ointment

VERY EARLY the next morning, Bob Andrews and Pete Crenshaw met in front of The Jones Salvage Yard. This establishment was owned by Jupiter's Uncle Titus and Aunt Mathilda Jones. It was a fascinating spot for anyone interested in curious old objects. Uncle Titus did most of the buying for the yard, and he had a talent for collecting unusual items along with ordinary junk. People came from all parts of Southern California to prowl through his finds. Wooden panelling rescued from houses which were to be torn down, ornate iron fences, marble mantles, old-fashioned, claw-legged bathtubs, odd brass doorknobs and hinges—all were to be found in Uncle Titus' stock. There was even a pipe organ, which Uncle Titus loved and refused to sell at any price.

When Bob and Pete arrived that December morning, no bargain hunters prowled through the heaps of salvage. In fact, the great iron gates of the yard were padlocked.

Pete yawned. "Sometimes I wish I'd never met Jupiter Jones," he announced. "Some nerve, calling at six in the morning!"

"No one ever said Jupe didn't have nerve!" Bob

remarked. "But if he called that early, we know it must be important. Come on."

The boys left the locked gate and walked along beside the board fence that surrounded the yard. This fence had been decorated by artists of Rocky Beach, for whom Uncle Titus had done favours from time to time. The front section featured a seascape—a stormy scene which showed a sailing ship foundering amid mountainous waves. In the foreground, a painted fish put its head out of the painted sea to watch the sinking ship. Bob pushed on the eye of the fish, and two green boards in the fence swung up. This was Green Gate One, a secret entrance to the salvage yard.

Bob and Pete went through the opening and let the gate swing shut behind them. They now stood in Jupiter's outdoor workshop, an area separated from the rest of the yard by carefully arranged heaps of junk. There was a small printing press in the workshop, and behind this was a piece of iron grating. Bob pulled the grating aside, bent down, and crawled into Tunnel Two, a length of corrugated pipe that ran beneath piles of salvaged iron to Headquarters.

Headquarters for the Three Investigators was a battered old mobile home trailer which stood at one side of the yard. It was hidden from view by heaps of old lumber and scrap iron.

Pete followed Bob into the tunnel, pulling the grating into place behind him, and crawled for forty feet. The pipe ended directly under a trap door in the floor of Headquarters.

"What took you so long?" asked Jupiter Jones when Bob pushed open the trap door. The chubby youth was in the tiny laboratory which the boys had fitted out.

Bob didn't answer, but Pete groaned as he climbed into the trailer. "I thought it would be nice if I brushed my teeth and put on some clothes before I came over," he said. "What's so important that we have to get up at dawn, and what have you got in that jar?"

Jupiter tilted the ceramic jar in his hand so that the others could see some fine white crystals.

"Magic powder," said Jupe.

Pete slumped into a chair and leaned sleepily against a file cabinet. "I hate it when you act mysterious," he said. "I especially hate it early in the morning."

Jupe took a flask of water from a shelf above the laboratory counter and poured a few drops over the white crystals, then stirred with a small plastic spoon. "These crystals are a metallic compound," he said. "I read about them in an old book on criminology. They will dissolve in water."

Bob sighed. "Are you going to give us a lecture on chemistry?"

"Perhaps." Jupe opened a drawer and took out a tube of thick, white ointment. He squeezed a good amount of this into the solution in the jar and then mixed everything slowly and thoroughly. "I've been holding this ointment for emergencies," he said proudly. "It will absorb water—not everything will."

29

He peered happily at the creamy paste in the jar. "That should do it," he announced as he screwed on a lid. "We now have a magic ointment."

"So what?" demanded Pete.

"Suppose we put a coating of this ointment on something . . . say, perhaps, the drawer handles of Mr Prentice's desk. The ointment will stay clean and white. But suppose someone then comes along and touches the drawer handles. Within half an hour, that person's fingers will have black spots on them—spots that cannot be washed away!"

"Aha!" said Bob. "You want us to take the case!"

"Mr Prentice called me late last night," said Jupe. "He said he couldn't get to sleep. Several times last evening he was sure that there was a shadowy presence in his apartment. He was upset and afraid."

"Good grief, Jupe, the man's a kook!" said Pete. "What can we do for him?"

"Yes, he could be imagining things," acknowledged Jupe. "I gather that he spends a great deal of time alone, and lonely people sometimes do imagine things. That's why I hesitated to take the case. But we may be doing him a great injustice if we don't investigate. He's right when he says that he can't take his problem to the police. He couldn't even take it to a regular firm of private investigators. If he's only imagining things, there may be nothing we can do for him. But if a real person is at the bottom of this, we may be able to identify him. I am sure it would be a great relief to Mr Prentice."

Jupiter looked at his companions. "Shall I call and tell him we'll come?"

Bob smiled. "You knew the answer to that before you called *us*," he said.

"Good," said Jupe. "The first bus from Rocky Beach to Los Angeles leaves at seven. I left a note for Aunt Mathilda saying that we won't be here this morning."

Pete handed him the Headquarters telephone. "Then call Mr Prentice and let's go," he said. "I don't want to be around when your aunt finds that note. You heard her talking yesterday. She has lots of plans for you—and none of them include smearing magic ointment around somebody's apartment!"

4

The Demon Dog

IT WAS ALMOST eight when the Three Investigators got off the Wilshire bus and walked up Paseo Place. Father McGovern, the pastor of St Jude's Church, was in front of the rectory fumbling in his pocket as they came along. He nodded cheerfully and wished them a good morning.

They did not encounter the unpleasant Mrs Bortz when they went into Mr Prentice's building, but they did not find the old gentleman at home, either. They found a note on his door, instead.

"My three young friends," read the note. "I am at 329 Lucan Court. The house is directly behind this building. Cross the alley and come around to the front door. I will be expecting you."

Jupe stuffed the note into his pocket. "That's the place that was broken into," he said.

"What are you boys doing up there?"

The boys looked down from the balcony and saw that Mrs Bortz had come out of her apartment. She wore a dressing gown and her red hair was tousled.

"Isn't Mr Prentice at home?" she asked.

"Apparently not," said Jupiter.

"Where could he be at this hour?" she said.

The boys didn't answer her. Instead they went down the stairs, through the courtyard, and out through the back entrance of the building—a little passageway that led past a laundry and a storeroom and up a few steps to an alley. They saw dustbins and garages and the backs of the buildings which faced the next street.

As Fenton Prentice had reported, 329 Lucan Court was directly behind Prentice's apartment house. It was a square, one-storey frame residence. When Pete rang the front doorbell, the door was opened by Charles Niedland, the grey-haired man who had been talking to Prentice the night before. He looked haggard.

"Come in." He stepped back and swung the door wide.

The Three Investigators entered a place that was partly a home and partly a studio. A skylight had been cut into the living room ceiling. The room had no carpets and very little furniture. There were drawing tables and an easel. Photographs and sketches were tacked all over the walls, and books were piled everywhere. There was also a tiny television set, a sophisticated-looking stereophonic sound system, and a huge collection of records.

Fenton Prentice sat on a daybed with his chin in his hands. He seemed tired but calm. "Good morning, boys," he said. "Perhaps you would like to solve another puzzle. As it turns out, *I* was the one who was robbed last night."

"Now, Fenton," said Charles Niedland. "I'm sure that was only an accident. No doubt the police scared the burglar off before he could take anything besides the Carpathian Hound "

Niedland turned to the boys. "Mr Prentice tells me that you have a knack for detection. I think, in this case, there is nothing unusual to detect. The burglar got in through the kitchen window. He used a glass cutter to make a hole in the windowpane and reached in and opened the latch. Very ordinary."

"But he took only the Carpathian Hound," insisted Prentice.

"The police didn't think that was odd," countered Charles Niedland. "They said the television set wouldn't be worth a darn, anyway. It's only a nine-inch screen. And the stereo had my brother's social security number etched on the underside of the turntable and on the speakers. That would make it very difficult to sell. Nothing else here is valuable. My brother lived very simply."

"A great artist," said Mr Prentice. "He lived for his art."

"What's a Carpathian Hound?" asked Pete.

Charles Niedland smiled. "A dog. A dog that probably never existed except in the minds of a few superstitious people. My brother was a romantic, and he liked to depict romantic subjects in his work.

"There's a legend that two centuries ago, a village in the Carpathian Mountains was haunted by a demon dog. I believe the Carpathian Mountain villagers are noted for being superstitious."

Jupiter nodded knowingly. "The area is also known as Transylvania. The vampire Dracula is supposed to have lived there."

"Yes," said Charles Niedland, "but the demon dog wasn't a vampire, or a werewolf, either. The people in the village believed he was the ghost of a nobleman—a man who was an avid hunter, and who bred a pack of savage hunting dogs. They were said to be part wolf. The nobleman wanted them to be keen when they hunted, so he kept the dogs half-starved. According to the old tale, one of the dogs got out of the kennel one night and killed a child."

"Oh, no!" exclaimed Bob.

"Yes. A tragedy, if it really did occur. The father of the child demanded that the dogs be destroyed. The nobleman refused, and it's said that he tossed a few coins to the villager as payment for the dead child. The father was very angry, of course, and in his rage he picked up a stone and hurled it at the nobleman. It killed him, but not instantly. Before he died, the vicious nobleman cursed the village and everyone in it. He vowed that he would return to haunt the place."

"I suppose he came back as a dog?" said Pete.

"A huge hound," said Charles Niedland. "A huge, half-starved hound who could have been part wolf. The nobleman's entire hunting pack was destroyed, but on dark nights, one gaunt creature roamed the streets, howling and whining, its ribs showing through its coat. The people were frightened. Some put out food for the beast, but it couldn't or wouldn't eat. So, if the demon dog *was* the old nobleman, the curse came true. He did haunt the village. However, there was a horrible justice to it, for he was always hungry, as his own dogs had always been.

"In time, the villagers moved away. If the dog still prowls, he does so in an abandoned ruin."

"Did your brother make a painting of the dog?" asked Jupe.

"My brother was not a painter," explained Charles Niedland. "He sketched, of course, when he was working out his designs, but he was really a sculptor. He worked in glass and crystal— sometimes in crystal combined with metals."

"The Carpathian Hound was a marvellous piece," said Fenton Prentice. "Edward Niedland made it especially for me. It was finished a month ago but never delivered. Edward was having a show of some of his newer work at the Maller Gallery, and he wanted to include the Hound. Of course I was happy to let him do so. And now it's gone!"

"It's a glass statue of a dog, then," said Bob.

"Crystal," Mr Prentice corrected him. "Crystal and gold."

"Crystal *is* a type of glass," Charles Niedland put in, "but an extremely special type. It's made of the very finest silica, with a high proportion of lead oxide, so it's heavier and much more brilliant than ordinary glass. My brother worked with glass—and crystal—that was so hot it was still almost liquid. He'd shape it with tools, then reheat it as it cooled, then shape it some more, reheat it, shape it, and so on until he had the form he wanted. Then he'd finish it, grinding and buffing and polishing with acid. When it was done, the Carpathian Hound was a magnificent sculpture. The eyes of the dog were rimmed with gold, and there was golden froth on the jowls. In the legend, the ghost dog was supposed to have glowing eyes."

"Perhaps you'll get it back." Bob sounded hopeful. "A thing like that would be difficult to sell."

"Not to anyone who had no scruples and who knew Edward Niedland's work," said Prentice. "He was so young . . . so talented. There are people who would happily consort with thieves to get their hands on one of his creations."

Jupe looked around the simple house. "Did he work here?" he asked. "Wouldn't he need a furnace to work with molten glass?"

"My brother had a workshop in East Los Angeles," said Charles Niedland. "That's where he actually executed his work."

"Weren't there any other sculptures here?" asked Jupe. "Did your brother keep none himself? Or were they at the workshop?"

"Edward had a small collection, of his own work and other artists', which he kept here at the house. I removed the pieces to a safer place after he died. It was pure chance that the Carpathian Hound was here when the burglar broke in."

Fenton Prentice sighed.

"You see," Charles Niedland continued, "my brother's gallery show ended several days ago. He had borrowed pieces for it from other patrons, too, and I have been returning them. Late yesterday afternoon I came here, intending to deliver the Carpathian Hound to Fenton and spend some time sorting out my brother's books. I arrived just when Fenton was expecting you boys—he'd told me about you earlier in the day, when I called to make arrangements. So I left the Hound and went out for a bite to eat first. When I came back, I saw through the window that an intruder was in the house. I called the police immediately from a neighbour's phone."

"Really, Charles, you were a little careless," said Mr Prentice with a trace of bitterness.

"Now, Fenton, let's not quarrel," answered Niedland. "Let's just call it bad luck."

"Did anyone else know the Hound was to be delivered yesterday?" asked Jupe.

Both men shook their heads.

"Was the Hound insured?" asked Bob.

"Yes, but what use is that when it can't be replaced?" replied Prentice. "It's . . . why, it's like losing the Mona Lisa! You can't be repaid for a thing like that."

"I assume the police looked for fingerprints and that sort of thing?" said Jupe.

"They were here half the night dusting fingerprint powder around," replied Niedland. "Apparently they found nothing conclusive. They are now checking their files of known criminals in case a specialist in art theft is involved."

"I'm sure they'll be very thorough," said Jupiter. "I doubt that there is more we could do."

Mr Prentice nodded, took his leave of Charles Niedland, and led the boys back through the alley and into the courtyard of his building. Mrs Bortz was there, picking a dead leaf off a plant. Mr Prentice ignored her and went upstairs with the boys trailing him.

Once they were in Prentice's apartment, with the door locked, Jupiter produced his jar of ointment and explained his plan. "There are ceramic knobs on your desk drawers," he told Mr Prentice. "They are perfect for our purpose. This chemical reacts with metal and might damage copper or brass, but it can't hurt ceramics. We'll coat the knobs with the ointment, then go out. If someone comes in here while we're away and opens a desk drawer, he will get black stains on his hands."

"The intruder seems able to come and go whether I am here or not," said Prentice. "Also, he seems able to ignore solid walls and doors. Why should a drawer handle bother him?"

"Mr Prentice, we can at least try it," said Jupe. "You told us that you once came home and found that your desk had been gone through."

"Very well," said Prentice. "I am willing to try anything. Anoint the drawer handles, and then let's go and get something to eat."

"Wonderful!" cried Pete. "I'm starved!"

Jupe applied his magic ointment to the knobs

on Prentice's desk drawers, using a paper towel to get the ointment out of the jar. Then he and Pete and Bob went out with Mr Prentice and walked slowly down the stairs, talking loudly of the place where they would eat. The courtyard was empty, but at the gate they encountered Mrs Bortz and the lank young man named Sonny Elmquist. Both were looking down towards the church.

An ambulance was at the church door.

"What happened?" asked Pete.

"It's the caretaker at the church," said Elmquist. "He's been hurt! The pastor found him a little while ago up in the choir loft!"

5

The Guilty Stains

THE THREE INVESTIGATORS and Mr Prentice rushed next door to the church. Two men in white were just coming out with a stretcher. On it lay Earl, the caretaker, covered to the chin with a blanket.

Father McGovern came out together with the vocal Mrs O'Reilly.

"He's killed!" the woman wailed. "Killed! Murdered! Dead!"

"Mrs O'Reilly, he's not dead, thanks be to God!" The priest was pale. His hands shook as he locked the church door. "I should have come back here with him last night and helped him close up. It isn't the first time he's fallen, but to have him lie in the choir loft all night!"

The priest came down the steps. "It's my fault for giving him his own way," he said. "He turns out most of the lights when he can and goes groping about in the gloom. He thinks he's saving money for the parish."

"Precious little he'll save on *this* piece of foolishness," said Mrs O'Reilly. "And who's to do his work while he's idling away his time in the hospital?"

"Now, don't you worry about that, Mrs O'Reilly," said the priest. "Why don't you go

41

and . . . and make yourself a nice cup of tea?" He got into the back of the ambulance. The doors closed and the vehicle started away from the kerb.

"Cup of tea!" exclaimed Mrs O'Reilly. "A nice cup of tea, he says! What ails the man? Earl with a hole knocked in his head, murdered perhaps by that wandering spirit, and he talks of cups of tea!"

She brushed past Prentice and the Three Investigators and went muttering towards the parish house.

"Murdered by a wandering spirit?" said Bob.

"She likes to think there's a ghost in the neighbourhood," said Fenton Prentice. "She claims she's seen one—the ghost of the former pastor. He's been dead for three years. She claims he appears in the church and on the street."

The boys and Mr Prentice walked on toward Wilshire Boulevard.

"Ah, Mr Prentice, do you suppose that this wandering spirit could be the same shadow that you see in your apartment?" asked Bob.

"Certainly not!" answered Mr Prentice. "I would recognize the ghost of the old pastor—if there is such a thing. So far, only Mrs O'Reilly has seen him. She insists that he walks about the church at night carrying a candle. Why he would be compelled to do that, I cannot imagine. He was a pleasant old man. I used to play chess with him. He wasn't given to night-walking. In fact, he was usually in bed by ten."

Mr Prentice and the boys turned the corner on

to Wilshire Boulevard and walked a few blocks to a private club. Inside, brass doorknobs gleamed with the lustre of years of care, the tablecloths were starched, and the carnation in the vase on the centre of their table was unmistakably real. It was late for breakfast and early for lunch. Except for a waiter who hovered near the door to the kitchen, they had the dining room to themselves.

"Mr Prentice," said Jupiter when they had been served, "your apartment building is rather large, but I haven't seen many people there. There is Mrs Bortz . . ."

Mr Prentice made an unpleasant face.

"Mrs Bortz," repeated Jupiter. "Also Sonny Elmquist. He seems to be home at odd hours."

"He works from midnight to morning at the market on Vermont," said Prentice. "Strange young person. There's something pathetic about a grown man who is called Sonny. I understand that his real name is Cedric. He has the smallest apartment in the building. I don't suppose he makes much money. There is also a young woman named Chalmers—Gwen Chalmers—who has the apartment next to Elmquist's. You haven't met her. She works as a buyer for a department store downtown. Mr Murphy is a stockbroker."

"He's the man who came up the steps last night after the police left," said Bob.

"Yes. He has the corner apartment at the back of the building. You may see him later today. He goes into his office very early, because the stock market opens early in New York and we're three hours behind the East Coast. He could be at home any time after noon. His nephew Harley Johnson, a college student, is with him at the moment. I understand Murphy is Harley's guardian. Then there's Alex Hassell, the cat man."

"Cat man?" echoed Pete.

Fenton Prentice smiled. "I tend to think of him that way. You see, he feeds cats. Every evening at five all the stray cats in the neighbourhood gather at his door and he feeds them. He also keeps a pet Siamese in his apartment."

"What does he do when he's not feeding cats?" asked Pete.

"Mr Hassell has no job," said Prentice. "He has private means, so he comes and goes as he pleases. I believe he walks through the city looking for stray cats to feed. If they're sick or injured, he takes them to a vet."

"Who else lives in your building?" asked Jupiter.

"A number of unremarkable people. There are twenty units in all. Most of the tenants are single people and most of them work. Also, most of them are away for the holidays, visiting friends or relatives. At the moment, only six of us are in residence. Seven, if you count Mr Murphy's nephew, Harley."

"That narrows our list of suspects," said Jupe.

Prentice looked searchingly at Jupe. "So you think that someone in the building is spying on me?"

"I won't be entirely sure until we get more evidence," answered Jupe. "But most likely the culprit is someone who would know when you're not at home. If he saw us leave this morning, he may have taken the opportunity to prowl around."

Mr Prentice shrugged. "Perhaps you're right, Jupiter. If anyone wanted to open my desk this morning, he has had ample time to do so."

Prentice signalled to the waiter to bring the check, and signed it. The Three Investigators followed him out of the club and along Wilshire to Paseo Place. The street was empty as they came up past the church. They reached the apartment house and went up the steps. In the apartment near the gate, where Mrs Bortz lived, they could hear water running and dishes clattering in a sink.

"Thank heavens that woman has to eat occasionally," said Prentice, "or we would *never* have a moment's privacy."

Pete laughed. "She does seem to be around a lot."

"A born busybody and a dreadful gossip," said Prentice. "She asks the most impertinent questions. She is even capable of going through the dustbins. I have surprised her at it more than once. I would have guessed it even if I hadn't seen it. How else would she know that Miss Chalmers eats frozen dinners or that Mr Hassell's group of stray cats consumes more than forty cans of pet food a week?"

The Three Investigators trailed Prentice to his apartment and he unlocked the door.

"Now, don't touch anything," cautioned Jupe. He took a small magnifying glass out of his pocket and went into the den, where he peered at the drawer handles of the desk.

"Aha!" he said.

Fenton Prentice came as far as the door.

"Someone has opened this desk since we left this morning!" Jupiter reported. "Someone with ordinary, solid, human hands. The ointment is smeared."

Bob went to the kitchen and got a paper towel, and Jupe wiped the handles clean.

"May we open the desk?" he asked Prentice.

"Of course."

Jupiter pulled out the top drawer. "Is anything missing?"

"There's never anything missing," said Prentice, "but someone has looked at that bill from the telephone company. It was at the back of the drawer this morning."

"Whoever moved it smudged the envelope. He must have gotten a good dose of the ointment on his hands." Jupe beamed with satisfaction.

Jupe went out through the living room to the front door. He stooped and peered at the door-knob.

"I didn't put any ointment on this knob," he reminded his friends, "but there are smudges on it now."

"So we know how the uninvited snooper left," said Bob. "He opened the door and walked out."

"And locked the dead bolt lock behind him,"

said Jupe. He opened the door and examined the dead bolt lock from the outside. It showed traces of the ointment. "Yes," he said. "Someone has a key."

"Impossible!" exclaimed Fenton Prentice. "That is a special lock which I had installed. No one could have a key!"

"Someone does," insisted Jupe.

The door was closed again, and the boys and Mr Prentice continued their examination of the apartment. There were more smudges on the edge of the mirror in the bathroom.

"The intruder looked into your medicine cabinet," Jupe told Mr Prentice.

Mr Prentice made an outraged sound.

"Well, at least we are making progress," said Jupiter.

"Are we?" asked Prentice.

"Certainly." Jupiter's voice was confident. "We know that the presence that haunts you cannot open a drawer without getting smudges on his fingers. He also left here this morning in the usual way, by opening the apartment door. We will go and sit in the courtyard and watch, and presently we will know who it is."

"Suppose it isn't anybody who lives here?" asked Prentice.

"I'm sure it *is* someone who lives here," said Jupe. "Someone who saw us leave this morning."

The boys left Prentice and went down to the courtyard. They took chairs beside the pool and waited.

"That's a fantastic swimming pool," remarked Pete after a bit.

Bob crouched at the edge and looked down through the clear water. Blue and gold tiles were set in a random arrangement at the bottom of the pool. "Very fancy. Reminds me of the indoor pool in the Hearst Castle in San Simeon." He put his hand into the water and reported that it was heated.

Footsteps sounded on the flagstone stairs and the front gate opened. A grey cat scampered into the court, followed by a tawny-haired man in a white sweater and a camel-coloured jacket. He looked at the boys without interest as he crossed the court to a door at the rear. The cat ran after him but was left outside when the man went into his apartment. In a few seconds he was back with a plate of food, which he put down on the flagstones. He stayed, crouching, while the cat devoured the food.

"Hassell," whispered Bob. "He was leaving when we arrived last night."

"He must have found a new stray," decided Pete. "One who doesn't know that five o'clock is dinner-time."

The cat finished eating and padded away. Hassell took the empty dish into his apartment.

There were more footsteps on the front stairs and again the gate opened. The robust, middle-aged man named Murphy came in. He was smoking a cigarette. He nodded to the boys, smiled, and made for his apartment, which was next to Hassell's. Before he reached it, the door opened. A youth who appeared to be in his late teens stood in the doorway scowling.

"Uncle John, can't you go ten seconds without a cigarette?" the boy demanded.

"Harley, don't nag. I've had a rough day. Where's my ashtray?"

"I washed it and put it out by the pool. The whole place stank with smoke."

Murphy turned and strode back to a table near the boys. He threw himself down in a chair, flicked some ashes into a big, bowl-shaped ashtray on the table, and continued to smoke his cigarette.

"I hope you kids don't give your folks a hard time like that," he said to the boys.

"My parents don't smoke," said Pete.

Murphy grunted. "I probably shouldn't either," he confessed. "Well, at least I'm careful. Don't burn holes in things. I've got another ashtray like this at my office. Even if I forget a cigarette and let it burn down, it can't fall out."

He carefully stubbed out his butt, got up, and carried the ashtray to his apartment.

When Murphy had gone, Pete looked across the pool to the apartment occupied by Sonny Elmquist. "I wonder if Elmquist is home," he said. "The curtains are drawn. Suppose we rang the doorbell and—"

"Wait!" Jupiter Jones sat up straight.

Mrs Bortz had come into the courtyard. She was rubbing at her hands with a bit of tissue. "Children are not allowed in the pool area without

49

an adult in attendance," she scolded.

Jupiter did not bother to answer. He merely stood up and went to her.

"Mrs Bortz, may I see your hands?" he asked.

"What?"

"Your hands, Mrs Bortz!" Jupe's voice was louder now.

A door opened above and Mr Prentice came out on to the balcony.

"There are black marks on your hands!" said Jupiter.

Fenton Prentice started down the stairs.

"Why . . . why, yes," said Mrs Bortz. "I must have gotten into something in the kitchen."

"You have been in Mr Prentice's apartment," said Jupiter sternly. "You have opened his desk and looked at his mail and even opened his medicine cabinet.

"*You* are the spy!"

6

The Mystery of the Mandala

FOR ONCE IN HER LIFE Mrs Bortz was at a loss for words. She stood gaping at Jupiter, her face growing redder and redder.

"It's no use rubbing your hands," said Jupe. "The stains won't come off."

Mr Prentice appeared behind the boys and said, "I'd like a word with you, Mrs Bortz."

The sound of his voice seemed to bring the manager back to her senses. She turned to Prentice and screeched, "Do you know what these horrid boys called me?"

"Yes, and they're quite right!" answered Prentice. "However, this need not become the concern of everyone in the building." He took a step towards the manager's apartment. "We'll discuss this in private."

"I . . . I'm busy," said the woman. "I . . . I have a great deal to do, as you know."

"Of course you do, Mrs Bortz," said Mr Prentice. "What were you planning just now? An inspection of the dustbins in the alley? An invasion of someone else's apartment? Come, Mrs Bortz. We will go inside and have a chat. Or would you like me to call my lawyer?"

Mrs Bortz gasped, but she went into her apartment.

Mr Prentice smiled at the Three Investigators. "I think I shall handle this myself," he told them, "but I would appreciate it if you would wait."

He followed Mrs Bortz into the apartment and closed the door behind him.

Jupe, Pete, and Bob remained in the courtyard. silent for a few minutes. They could hear Mrs Bortz's voice, high and angry, but they couldn't hear what she was saying. At intervals she was silent, and the boys could imagine Mr Fenton Prentice, soft-spoken but sure, and possibly threatening.

"He's a nice old guy," said Pete, "but I bet he can be tough on anybody who steps on his toes."

A door across the pool cracked open, and Sonny Elmquist came out, blinking in the sunshine. He wore a pair of tattered denims, a shirt with several buttons missing, and no shoes. He yawned.

"Good morning," said Jupiter.

Elmquist blinked and rubbed his eyes. The boys could see that he hadn't washed his face or combed his hair.

"Um!" he said. He almost stumbled when he walked away from his open door. He seemed to have some trouble deciding whether he would sit down in one of the chairs near the boys, or whether he would simply stand and stare limply into the swimming pool.

He finally did neither. He sat on the flagstone

decking, crossed his legs, and tucked his feet up over his thighs. Jupiter recognized the posture; it was the lotus position used by students of yoga.

"Good morning," said Jupiter again.

The young man turned his pale face to Jupe and stared at him for a second. His eyes were of no particular colour. The whites were bloodshot, as if he had not slept enough.

"It's still morning?" he said.

Jupe looked at his watch. "In fact, it isn't. It's after one."

Sonny Elmquist yawned again.

"Mr Prentice tells me that you work at the all-night market over on Vermont," said Jupe.

Elmquist became a little more alert. He smiled. "Midnight to morning," he said. "It's a rough shift sometimes, but they pay extra if you're willing to keep those hours. And when we're not busy, I can study."

"You're going to school?" asked Jupiter.

Sonny Elmquist waved a hand, as if schools were a complete waste of time. "Finished that long ago," he told the boys. "My old man wanted me to go to college, be a dentist just like him. Couldn't see it. Stand around on your feet all day poking at people's molars, getting a crick in your back. What for? It's all an illusion, anyway."

"An illusion?" said Pete.

"Yeah. Everything's an illusion. The whole world. We're all like a bunch of sleepers having a bad dream. Me, I'm going to wake up!"

"What are you studying?" said Jupe.

"Meditation," said Elmquist. "That's the way to reach the Ultimate Consciousness." He unfolded his legs and stood up, obviously pleased to have an audience.

"I'm saving my money," he said. "I want to go to India to find a guru. The best teachers are there. So I work nights, because I get more per hour. Pretty soon I'll have enough to get to India and stay three or four years, or however long it takes to know . . . to really know everything. Oh, not that I want to know all about science or anything like that, because that's useless. I want to know how to not want anything. That's the only worthwhile thing, don't you think?"

Bob said doubtfully, "Well, yes, I suppose if you don't want anything . . . if you have everything you want . . ."

"No, no. You don't understand!" exclaimed Elmquist.

"I'm not sure I want to!" muttered Pete.

"It's very simple. Desire, wanting things, that's where all our troubles begin. Like old Prentice, all he does is worry about his possessions—his collection. In his next life he'll probably be a . . . a pack rat!"

"Hey, now!" exclaimed Pete. "He's a nice old man."

Sonny Elmquist shook his head. "I don't mean he'd steal or hurt anybody to get things, only he *cares* so much about what he has and he always wants more. He'll never understand that he's just chasing after something that's not real. Do you know he has a mandala and doesn't even know how to use it? He just hangs it on his wall as if it were another painting."

"What's a mandala?" asked Pete.

Elmquist darted into his apartment and was back in a moment with a little book. "I'd love to have one," he said eagerly. "It's a kind of diagram of the cosmos. If you meditate on it, all the illusory things of life fade away and you become one with the universe." He opened the book and showed a colourful drawing composed of overlapping triangles which were surrounded by a circle. The circle, in its turn, was edged about by a square.

"I don't remember seeing anything like that in Mr Prentice's apartment," said Pete.

"His is more complicated," explained Elmquist. "His is from Tibet, and it shows some of the old deities that used to be worshipped there."

Elmquist closed the little book. "I'm going to have my own mandala one day," he said. "It will be designed for me by a guru. Now I just use the television."

"Huh?" said Bob.

"The television," repeated Elmquist. "It helps me get detached. I mean, I come home after spending all night checking people out at the market and making sure my register tallies, and I'm really fenced in. So I turn on the TV, but I don't turn on the sound, see? Then I stare at a place in the middle of the screen, or maybe in one corner of the screen. I don't even try to notice what's happening—I just look at the patterns of colour. Pretty soon I'm really away from the market, from everything. I'm not even here."

"You're asleep," accused Bob.

Elmquist looked slightly abashed. "That's . . . that's the trouble with meditation," he admitted. "Sometimes I get so peaceful that I do fall asleep and dream, only . . ."

He stopped talking. Mr Prentice had come out of Mrs Bortz's apartment and stood at the foot of the stairs, looking towards the Three Investigators.

"I'm sorry," said Jupiter to Elmquist. "We have to go."

"Well, drop around any time I'm home," said Elmquist eagerly. "If I'm not meditating, you know. I'll be glad to tell you more about the mandala, and the . . . the trip I'm going to take."

The boys thanked him and went to Prentice.

When they were inside Prentice's apartment, the old gentleman sat down on one of his big low chairs.

"Mrs Bortz had a key to this apartment, didn't she?" prompted Jupe.

"Yes, she did," admitted Prentice. "You were right when you said at the very beginning that there had to be a second key. That wretched woman! I have a special clause in my lease stipulating that my apartment is *never* to be entered by the manager. I may contact the Martin Company, which owns this building."

"How did she get the key?" asked Bob.

"Very easily. When I was in Europe two months

ago, she called a locksmith who often works for her. He wouldn't question her authority. She told him she had lost the key for this lock, and that she had to get into the apartment to check for a leak in a pipe. He removed the lock and had a key made for her, then replaced the lock."

" A curious woman," said Jupiter.

"Curious to the point of mania," agreed Fenton Prentice. "Well, that solves the mystery of who has been poking through my desk and snooping into my papers. Naturally, I took the key from her. I am most grateful to you young men."

Mr Prentice smiled shyly at the boys and added, "You know, I'm quite relieved to learn that Mrs Bortz was my intruder. I mean, that a real human being was coming in here. I think I must have imagined that shadowy presence. Really, it's too ridiculous! I was so upset at the idea of someone invading my home, I must have been a little out of my mind! Mrs O'Reilly's ghost stories probably gave me ideas." He shook his head, as if amazed at his own folly.

Jupe sat pinching his lower lip—a sign that he was thinking hard—and stared thoughtfully at the old man. Finally he smiled and said, "Well, that's settled then. We're happy to have been of service." He got up to go. "Incidentally, Mr Prentice, do you own a mandala ?"

"Why, yes. How did you know? Would you like to see it ?"

At Jupe's nod, the man led the way into the den and pointed out a framed design that hung on the wall over the desk. It was intricate and brightly coloured. A circle decorated with drawn scrollwork enclosed a square. Oriental deities or demons appeared in the four corners of the picture. The centre was composed of triangles overlapping triangles, intersecting one another and enclosing smaller circles in which tiny beings had been depicted.

Prentice said, "This belonged to a young artist I once knew who had travelled to Tibet. It was made especially for him. That was long ago. He has been dead for many years, and I acquired the mandala from his estate. I always admired it as a piece of design, although I know little of Eastern religions."

"Mr Prentice, has Sonny Elmquist ever been in this apartment?" asked Jupiter Jones.

"Certainly not," said Prentice. "Except for that malignant specimen of womanhood who manages this place, no one else in the building has ever been here. I value my privacy, as you know. Least of all would I open the door to young Elmquist. He has a lot of half-baked ideas, and he doesn't seem particularly clean."

"No, he doesn't," agreed Jupe. "Have you had any occasion to send the mandala out for repair? Has it been framed lately, for example?"

Prentice shook his head. "It's been hanging on that wall for more than ten years. It has only been taken down when the apartment has been painted. Why?"

"How would Sonny Elmquist know that you

own a mandala?"

"He knows that?"

"He does. He even knows that it's a Tibetan mandala. He has a book with a diagram somewhat like it, but much simpler."

Prentice shrugged. "I can only guess that those tiresome newspapers mentioned I have a mandala in my collection. My friends in the art world know of it."

Jupe nodded and headed for the door.

"Now, Jupiter," said Mr Prentice jovially. "Don't you go looking around here for another mystery! One was quite enough!"

"You're right, Mr Prentice," agreed Jupe. "And I'm glad we could solve it for you. Feel free to call on us if you have any problems in the future."

"I will, boys, I will." Mr Prentice shook hands all around and ushered the Investigators out.

The boys trooped downstairs and out to the street.

"Well, that's that!" exclaimed Pete as they headed for their bus stop. "Must be the quickest case we ever solved! Now what are we going to do for the rest of Christmas vacation?"

"Stay out of The Jones Salvage Yard for one thing," retorted Bob. "Aunt Mathilda is all too willing to fill up our time! You're in for it now, Jupe!"

"Mmmnpf," replied Jupe. His mind was on something else, and he hardly spoke a word all the way home to Rocky Beach.

As the boys parted outside the junkyard,

Jupiter suddenly said, "Please stay close to your telephones, fellows. The Investigators may have more work to do soon. I don't think we've heard the last from Fenton Prentice!"

He smiled mysteriously and waved good-bye.

7

The Light in the Church

AUNT MATHILDA began scolding the minute she saw Jupiter enter the salvage yard.

"You went off this morning without so much as a by-your-leave! Writing a note and pinning it to your pillow is not at all the same as telling me where you'll be! Jupiter, I had things planned—"

"It's always slow at the salvage yard after Christmas," Jupe pointed out. "And I'm free now. I can work for the rest of the day."

"See that you do," grumbled Aunt Mathilda. "Your uncle just brought in a whole load of small appliances. Sort them out and see what works and what can be fixed. I suppose you'll end up buying half of them yourself."

Jupiter grinned. He was always on the lookout for junk that could be fashioned into detective equipment. Headquarters was full of devices that he had repaired or rebuilt from odd parts—walkie-talkies, a loudspeaker for the phone, a tape recorder, a periscope. Most of the money that Jupe earned by working in the yard went into these items.

For the rest of the afternoon, Jupe happily sorted through his uncle's latest acquisitions, setting aside a few things that he thought he could use. At six he walked across the street to the Jones house for dinner. An hour later the phone rang.

Aunt Mathilda answered it and announced, "It's for you, Jupiter."

Jupe's eyes gleamed as he took the receiver.

"Jupiter? Is that you?" said a quavery voice. "Fenton Prentice here. Jupiter, you won't believe this, but . . . but my apartment is still being haunted!"

"Yes," replied Jupe calmly.

"After you trapped that Bortz woman, I was sure I'd imagined that shadowy presence," Prentice went on. "But I didn't! I just saw it again, in my den! Either I'm losing my mind or I *am* being haunted!"

"Would you like us to come into town this evening?"

"Please. In fact, I'd deem it a favour if you and your friends would stay overnight with me. I don't usually like company, but . . . well, I can't bear to be alone here! I sit wondering when that thing will appear next—and I can't stand it!"

"We'll be there as soon as we can," promised Jupiter.

"Jupiter, must you always be running off?" complained Aunt Mathilda as soon as he'd hung up. But when Jupe explained briefly about the Investigators' elderly, frightened client, Mrs Jones became sympathetic.

"Poor soul!" she said. "It's hard enough to be

old without being alone. You boys go stay with him as long as he wants. Your uncle can drive you into town."

Jupe called Pete and Bob, and before long the boys were piling into the back of Uncle Titus' small pick-up truck for the trip into Los Angeles.

"Well, Jupe, you did it again," said Pete as he settled into a comfortable position. "How did you know we'd hear more from Prentice?"

"Because I was sure he wasn't imagining that presence in his apartment. I saw it myself."

"You what?" exclaimed Bob. "When?"

"Yesterday, in Mr Prentice's den. I saw someone in there. At first I thought it was Pete, but he was in the living room."

"I remember," said Pete. "But you decided it was only a shadow."

"At the time, it seemed the only logical conclusion. Later, I was not so sure. As soon as I saw Sonny Elmquist—"

"You jumped," recalled Bob. "Elmquist came out of his apartment after the police arrived and you kind of jumped."

"Yes. Did you notice that he resembles Pete?" asked Jupe.

"Hey, now!" Pete protested. "I don't look anything like that guy. He's at least twenty, and he's skinny, and—"

"He's about as tall as you are," Jupe interrupted. "He has dark hair, as you do, and last night he was wearing a black sweater and you were wearing a dark jacket. The light in Mr Prentice's den was dim. I thought I saw you. Isn't it possible that I saw Sonny Elmquist?"

Bob and Pete sat still, pondering this. At last Bob said, "But how could he get in? The door was locked."

"I don't know," admitted Jupe. "I'm not even positive it was Elmquist I saw. But *somebody* besides Mrs Bortz has found a way into that apartment. Now *we* have to find an explanation."

Within an hour of his call, the Three Investigators were at Mr Prentice's door.

"Thank goodness you're here," Prentice said. "I am quite unnerved!"

"Understandably," replied Jupe. "May we look around?"

Prentice nodded and Jupe made a beeline for the den. The desk lamp cast a soft glow in one corner of the room, illuminating richly bound books on shelves, a few Chinese porcelains, and the mandala above the desk. Jupe stared up at the intricate design, frowning and pulling at his lip.

And again, as on the previous evening, he had the feeling that someone stood silently watching him.

Jupe spun around.

There was a sensation of a darker darkness which seemed to pulse, then ebb away, in the far corner of the room.

Jupe jumped towards that corner. His hands groped at walls—plain plaster walls. He switched on the overhead light and stared wildly around. No one else was there.

He dashed out to the front door, startling the others as he sped past, and went to the balcony.

Below in the courtyard, the swimming pool was a swirl of gold and blue, and the floodlights sent amber beams up against the walls of the building. Jupe could see the windows of Sonny Elmquist's apartment. The curtains were open. A bright flicker of movement indicated that the television set in Elmquist's living room was on. Jupe could see Elmquist himself sitting motionless on the floor, his head hanging slightly forward as if he had nodded off.

"What is it?" Bob whispered behind him.

"I saw him again," murmured Jupe. He found himself shivering, and he told himself bravely that it was only because of the evening chill. "In the den. I was in the den, looking at the mandala, and there was someone else there. I could have sworn it was Sonny Elmquist. But it couldn't be. Look—there he is in his own place. Even if there were a secret passage—some way to get into Mr Prentice's apartment—he wouldn't have had time to get back down. Not possibly."

Jupe looked over his shoulder at the doorway. Fenton Prentice stood there, visibly shaking.

"You saw him, didn't you?" said Prentice. "You saw him, so I am *not* going mad."

The boys went in and closed the door.

"No, Mr Prentice, you are not going mad," said Jupiter. "I saw him yesterday also, but I couldn't believe my eyes. Did you recognize him as Sonny Elmquist, too?"

"I couldn't be sure. The . . . the shape always went away so quickly. One can't make wild accusations. But I thought it was Elmquist."

"Yet how can it be him?" wondered Jupe. "The two times I saw the shadow, Elmquist was in his own apartment, seemingly asleep. How can he be in two places at once?" He shook his head in puzzlement. "Mr Prentice, what do you actually know about Elmquist?"

"Very little," said Prentice. "He has only lived here for about six months."

"Were you ever aware of the presence of this shadow, or whatever it is, before Elmquist arrived?" Jupe asked.

Prentice thought for a moment, then shook his head. "No. The experience is quite new to me."

"He is interested in your mandala," said Jupe. "Are you sure you never mentioned it to him?"

"Positive," said Prentice. "The young man does not have an engaging personality and I avoid him. Miss Chalmers has mentioned him to me on occasion. She is a sociable young woman, but she doesn't care for Elmquist, either. She swims every night, hoping to take off weight, and he often comes out and sits beside the pool and tries to strike up a conversation with her. She describes him as 'creepy.' "

"I know it doesn't seem possible, but there must be a secret passage," decided Bob.

"Unlikely," said Jupe, "but we might as well eliminate the possibility."

The boys searched then, beginning in the den.

They found no secret passage. The apartment building, while not new, was well constructed and the walls and floors were intact. There seemed no way anyone could enter the place without coming in through the door.

"Spooky," said Bob.

Prentice nodded. "I have lived here for a long time and I like this apartment, but I may have to look for another place to live. I cannot bear this feeling of being observed."

The haunting shadow did not appear during the rest of the evening. Prentice grew tired and withdrew to his bedroom. The boys decided to take turns keeping watch all night. Bob bedded down on the sofa in the living room, and Pete stretched out on a couch in the den.

Jupe, who had chosen to be first on watch, sat with his back to the front door and listened.

After eleven, there was little enough to listen to. The traffic sounds on the street had long since ceased; Paseo Place was not a main thoroughfare. Jupe was aware of a faint splashing sound that came to him through the door panels, and assumed that it was Miss Chalmers having her chilly nightly swim.

"Jupe?" Pete had come in from the den. "Come here! I want you to see something."

Jupe followed him to the window in the den. Pete pointed outside. "There's a light in the church," he said.

There was. The stained-glass window which was closest to Prentice's apartment glowed briefly with colour, then went dark again.

"Could be the pastor seeing that the place is locked," said Jupe. "Then again . . ."

"Then again, what?" asked Pete.

"Maybe it isn't the pastor. I'm going to check."

"I'll go with you," said Pete.

"No. You stay here and take over the guard on the door," ordered Jupiter. "I'll be right back."

Jupe found his jacket in the front closet, unlocked the door, and stepped out on to the balcony. The courtyard lights were off now, and the pool was empty. Jupe shivered and hurried downstairs.

When he reached the street, he saw the mysterious light flicker briefly in a window. Jupe went up the steps of the church and touched one of the doors. It was not even latched. He pushed, and it swung open in front of him.

He stepped into near darkness. There was one candle burning near the front of the church—a candle held by someone dressed in black. The candle flickered in the draft.

The person holding the light turned. Jupe had an impression of a very white face and a great deal of snow-white hair. He could not see the eyes of the man. They seemed to be hidden in the dark shadow of the sockets. Above the man's black clothing was a rim of white—a collar such as priests wear.

The man did not speak. He stood, staring across the candle flame at Jupiter Jones.

"I beg your pardon, Father," said Jupe. "I saw a light from outside and I wondered if everything was all right."

The man made a quick motion with his hand and snuffed out his candle.

"Father?" said Jupe. The church was completely dark. Jupe felt a prickle of fear at the base of his skull. He took a step backwards towards the door.

Then the door was caught by a draft and slammed shut behind him.

Suddenly Jupiter was shoved! He stumbled, caught his toe on a kneeling bench, and was shoved again. He went floundering down between two pews.

In the darkness, he heard the church door open. Then it slammed and the lock turned.

Jupe stumbled to his feet and felt his way to the door. He touched the handle, twisted it, and pulled.

The door rattled, but it didn't open.

Jupiter was locked in!

8

The Vanishing Saint

JUPE GROPED at the wall beside the church door. He felt a light switch under his hand and pressed on it. The overhead lights glowed.

Slowly, his eyes darting to left and right, Jupe moved nervously away from the door. He went down the aisle to the place where he had seen the pallid priest holding the candle.

There was no one there.

Quickly Jupe made a circuit of the church. A door led out from the left side of the altar to a small room which contained cupboards and drawers filled with linens and vestments. On the far side of the room was another door which, Jupe supposed, led to the outside of the church. It was locked firmly.

"I think," said Jupe to himself, "that it is time to create an uproar."

With that he hurried back to the front doors and began to beat on them. "Help!" he cried. "I'm locked in! Help!"

He stopped, listened a moment, then pounded again.

"Pete!" shouted Jupe. "Father McGovern! Help!"

Again he waited. And yelled and waited.

"Don't you be going in there, Father!" said a woman outside the church.

"Now, Mrs O'Reilly!" Jupe recognized the voice of Father McGovern. "I'd not be that foolish. The police will be here any minute and—"

"Father McGovern!" shouted Jupe. "It's Jupiter Jones! Someone locked me in!"

"Jupiter Jones?" The priest sounded puzzled.

Jupe heard a siren approaching from the direction of Wilshire. He leaned back against the door and again surveyed the church. The pastor, he was sure, would not unlock the door before the police arrived. Jupe knew that the interview with the police might be unpleasant. He stared down the aisle and frowned.

The siren came nearer and nearer, then abruptly ceased.

A key was inserted into the lock. The door opened.

The pastor stood there in a bathrobe next to Mrs O'Reilly. Her long, grey hair was in a braid that hung down over her shoulder.

"Stand aside, please." said a policeman behind her.

She took a step to the left, and Jupe stared into the eyes of a young patrolman. He was one of the men who had searched the church the night before. His partner, beside him, had a drawn gun.

"Well?" said the first officer.

Jupe pointed to the place where the white-haired priest had stood holding the candle.

"I saw a light in the church," he explained. "I ran over to investigate, and when I came in I saw a priest over there. Then someone knocked me down and went out and locked the door."

"You came over to investigate?" asked the second policeman.

"I was in Mr Prentice's apartment," said Jupe.

"Oh. Oh, yes!" said Father McGovern. "You were with Mr Prentice this morning, on the street. But you saw no priest in this church tonight. The church has been locked since six. My assistant is away. You couldn't have seen a priest in this church."

"Yes he could!" cried Mrs O'Reilly. "You know he could!"

"Mrs O'Reilly, the old pastor does *not* haunt this place," said the priest.

"Wait a second!" cried someone behind the policemen.

Pete had come down the pavement. With him was Fenton Prentice.

"That young man is my guest," said Mr Prentice. "He and his friends are staying overnight with me. This is Pete Crenshaw. He tells me that he woke a short time ago, and that he saw a light in the church. He called it to Jupiter's attention, and Jupiter went out to investigate."

The second officer looked with great disapproval from Jupe to Pete and then to Mr Prentice.

"It's bad enough for kids to play cops and robbers," he said, "without an adult trying to excuse them!"

Mr Prentice stiffened, then sniffed.

"But there *was* a light in the church," said Pete.

"And someone *was* here," added Jupe. "A man in dark clothes, with a white collar like the one you wear, Father McGovern. He had white hair. He was over there holding a candle."

"Tall story," replied the policeman. "And for your sake, kid, I hope there's nothing missing."

"Something *is* missing from the church," said Jupiter. "Something that was here last night."

He looked questioningly at the pastor. "There was a statue over there." He pointed. "Down that aisle, next to the window. It was a statue of someone wearing a green cape and a tall, pointed cap. He was holding a staff."

The two policemen crowded in through the doorway and stared. "By darn, he's right!" exclaimed the younger of the two. "Last night I was here and there *was* a statue over there—St Patrick, I guess. Isn't he the one who's always dressed in green, and he wears a bishop's hat—what do you call it?"

Father McGovern stared, too. "A mitre," he said softly. "St Patrick always wears a mitre and carries a bishop's staff."

"So what happened to the statue?" asked the puzzled young cop.

"There has never been a statue of St Patrick in this church," said Father McGovern. "This is the Church of St Jude. He's the patron saint of the impossible."

"That makes sense," said the second policeman

sarcastically. "Your housekeeper sees the ghost of the old priest, which is impossible, and this kid here sees him, too, which is impossible, and we see a statue here last night which has never been here, so that's impossible. I don't suppose you've got a bishop's hat tucked away someplace?"

Father McGovern started. "There was a bishop's mitre and a staff in the church yesterday," he said suddenly.

"How come?" asked the policeman.

"We had a pageant," explained the priest. "For Christmas, you know. The children put it on for the parents. They did it right in the church, the way the old plays were done in the Middle Ages. They had the Nativity scene and the three wise men, and then at the very end all the famous men of the church came in. St Patrick among them, of course. He's quite a favourite. We had a bishop's mitre for him, and a staff and a green cloak. I took them back to the costume house today."

"Aha!" said Jupiter Jones. "So that's what happened to the burglar!"

"Huh?" said one of the cops.

"It is perfectly logical," said Jupiter in his most superior manner. "Last night this neighbourhood was swarming with policemen, all of them searching for a man who had broken into a house on the next street. That man ducked into the church. When it appeared that the church would be searched, he quickly put on the cape and the mitre and posed as a statue. When you were looking in here for him, you were so close that

74

you could have touched him."

The two policemen stared.

"Naturally, he was startled when the caretaker came down from the choir loft," Jupe continued. "Possibly he became desperate when the caretaker returned to the church after the search. The caretaker would notice, wouldn't he, if there was a statue where none was supposed to be? Father McGovern, was the caretaker able to remember what happened when he hurt himself?"

The priest shook his head. "He thinks he stumbled. He has a bad concussion, and he's being treated for shock."

"He may have been struck," Jupe pointed out. "He turned out some of the lights, but even so, the burglar may have been afraid he'd be seen. He may have crept up behind the caretaker and—"

The priest put up a hand to stop Jupiter. "I should have come back here with him," he said. "Poor Earl!"

"I hate to think how this is going to look on a report," said one of the policemen. "A burglar who masquerades as a statue! A kid who says he saw a ghost!"

"I saw a man wearing dark clothes and a white collar," corrected Jupe. "I did not say I saw a ghost."

"How would a mortal man get in?" demanded the housekeeper. "The door was locked. You heard Father McGovern say so himself. It was the old one—poor restless soul!"

"He got in with a key," decided the second

officer. "He had to, because when he went out again he locked the door. Father McGovern, who has keys to the church?"

"I do, of course," said the pastor. "And Mrs O'Reilly . . . my assistant . . . Earl, of course. I suppose his are with his things at the hospital. And there's an extra set in the parish house, in case anyone loses his. In the coat closet in the downstairs hall. They're on a hook there."

"Are they, Father?" asked Jupiter.

Father McGovern turned and hurried down to the parish house. He was back in a few minutes.

"They're gone," he said.

No one spoke.

"It . . . it *is* a rather stupid place to leave a set of keys," the pastor admitted. "So many people come to the parish house for one thing or another. They often use the coat closet."

"What you're saying, Father," said one of the officers, "is that almost anyone in the neighbourhood could have gotten his hands on the keys to this church."

The pastor nodded glumly.

"We'd better call the lieutenant," said the older policeman. "He'll want to know that the burglar, alias the vanishing saint, came back here tonight as a phantom priest."

"That's not what happened," said Jupiter.

"You said you saw a guy in black clothes and a clerical collar," the policeman reminded him.

"I did. But he wasn't the one who pushed me down and locked the door on me. The person in black was down there, towards the front of the church. Whoever pushed me was here in the back. The 'phantom' wouldn't have had time after he put out his candle to get back here and out the door. Tonight there were *two* intruders in the church!"

"Two people!" The housekeeper moaned. "The old one, and one other." She turned on the pastor. "And don't you be telling me to go and make myself a nice cup of tea," she warned. "I'll not hear of it this night!"

9

The Burglar Calls!

THE THREE INVESTIGATORS spent the rest of the night keeping watch in the Prentice apartment. There were no shadowy visitors and no further disturbances. In the morning, Mr Prentice was astir early, scrambling eggs and making toast.

"Well, boys," he said as he served them breakfast, "have you come to any conclusions?"

"Yeah. I'm stumped!" said Pete.

"It's too soon to say that," reproved Jupiter. "Things are just beginning to get interesting. We have a great deal to think about."

"Like what?"

"Like the burglar. His use of the church next door intrigues me."

"That's all very well," said Mr Prentice. "But what has the burglar to do with the shadow in my apartment?"

"I don't know," admitted Jupe. "But I think there may be some connection. Mr Prentice, do you usually see the shadow at a particular time of day or night? I've seen him twice in the early evening. When do you see him?"

Fenton Prentice thought a moment. "Usually in the late afternoon or evening, I would say.

Perhaps earlier in the day once or twice."

"Never in the middle of the night?"

"I'm usually asleep then, but I don't recall seeing him the few times I've been awake late at night."

Jupe nodded. "If it's all right with you, then, we'd like to leave and come back later in the day. I have an idea for the next step in this case, one which will require some preparation in Rocky Beach. And I believe Pete and Bob have some chores to attend to. You'll be quite safe. The shadow is unlikely to appear before we return."

The boys finished breakfast and left. As they came down the stairs into the courtyard, Sonny Elmquist sprang up from a pool chair.

"Hey, I hear you saw the phantom priest!" he said to Jupe. "I wish you had stopped by last night and let me know. I'm interested in things like that."

"Let you know?" Jupe stared at Elmquist. "How could I let you know? You were at work, weren't you?"

"I had the night off last night," said Elmquist. "I don't work all the time. Who does?"

"How'd you know Jupe saw the phantom priest?" demanded Pete.

"Easy. Mrs O'Reilly told Mrs Bortz. Mrs Bortz told Hassell, and Hassell told me."

The boys went down the stairs to the street with Elmquist trailing them.

"No kidding?" said Elmquist. "You really saw him?"

79

"I saw someone," answered Jupe.

The boys left Elmquist in front of the building and went down the street to Wilshire. "That Elmquist is weird," said Pete when they were aboard the bus bound for Rocky Beach.

"Because he's interested in ghosts and mandalas and Oriental thought?" said Jupe. "That's not so unusual these days." He leaned back against his seat. "And you can't really argue with some of his ideas. All great religions teach that too much interest in wealth and possessions is a bad thing."

"The love of money is the root of all evil," quoted Bob.

"Exactly. But I know what you mean, Pete. There *is* something strange about Elmquist. And his apparent ability to walk through walls is a real mystery!"

By 9.30 the Three Investigators were back in Rocky Beach. "I think it's time we reviewed what we've learned," announced Jupe as the boys left the bus stop. "Let's go to Headquarters first."

Ten minutes later the Investigators were seated around the old desk in their trailer.

"We now have three mysteries to solve," said Jupe happily. "First, the shadow who haunts Mr Prentice. Who is he and how does he get into the apartment? Next, the burglar who stole the Carpathian Hound. Who is *he*, and why has he been using the church? Finally, the phantom priest. Who's that, and what, if anything, does he have to do with the other mysteries? Let's take them in order."

"I thought we already knew who the shadow was," said Pete. "Both you and Mr Prentice recognized Sonny Elmquist."

"True," acknowledged Jupiter. "But we only caught brief glimpses. I hope you fellows get to see the shadow for yourselves sometime."

"At least we know the shadow isn't Mrs Bortz," put in Bob. "She walked right in with a key!"

Jupe nodded. "And she's the wrong shape and size—much too heavy to be that skinny shadow person. Elmquist is the right build. But I just don't see how he could get into Mr Prentice's apartment. And how can a person be in two places at the same time? Both times I saw the shadow, Elmquist was asleep in his own apartment."

Pete shrugged. "So maybe the shadow is someone else."

"But Elmquist knew about the mandala," Bob pointed out. "He described it accurately, so he must have seen it somehow. And Mr Prentice certainly never invited him in."

"So Elmquist is our chief suspect for the shadow," concluded Jupe, "but we have no proof or explanation. Now, let's tackle the burglar. The evidence suggests that he is someone from Mr Prentice's neighbourhood—perhaps even from his own building—because he knew where to get a key to the church. Who in that neighbourhood knew about the Carpathian Hound and its value?"

"The shadow?" guessed Pete. "Maybe the shadow saw papers in Mr Prentice's desk or overheard a phone conversation."

"How about Mrs Bortz?" Bob suggested. "She could have seen papers referring to the Hound when she snooped in Mr Prentice's apartment."

"If *she* knew about the Hound, so did everyone in the neighbourhood!" exclaimed Pete.

"Jupe, do you think the burglar went to Niedland's house intending to steal the Carpathian Hound?" asked Bob.

"It's hard to say. How would he have known the Hound was there just then? Perhaps he just hoped to find something of value in the house. If he lived in the neighbourhood, he would know the house was vacant. So he broke in, found the sculpture, and was scared off by the police. He ran into the church and disguised himself as a statue of St Patrick. What nerve! To simply stand there in a cape and mitre while the police swarmed around!"

"Then the police left but the caretaker came back," continued Bob. "So the burglar knocked him out and escaped!"

"I think we can assume violence on the part of the burglar," agreed Jupe. "He'd know that, sooner or later, Earl would notice a brand new statue. It seems most likely that the burglar struck Earl, then hid the sculpture in the church and came back for it last night."

"But why?" asked Pete. "Why couldn't the burglar put it in his pocket or under his jacket the night he stole it? Why leave it in the church?"

"Too risky," answered Jupiter. "He might be

afraid that squad cars were still in the area. He might be afraid of being stopped and questioned and even searched. He'd guess it was safer to leave the Hound in the church for a day and retrieve it the next day."

"So he came back last night as the phantom priest," said Pete.

"No, I don't think so," said Jupe. "The phantom priest was simply standing down by the altar when I saw him. The crook would have gone directly to the hiding place of the crystal dog and then left immediately. I think he must have been leaving when I came in. He gave me a shove to get me out of the way and ran out, locking the door behind him."

"Then who was the phantom priest?" asked Bob.

"Sonny Elmquist?" suggested Pete. "He likes ghosts, and he was home last night. Maybe he's in cahoots with the burglar."

"That would be an unlikely combination," said Jupe. "A man who is interested in separating himself from worldly desires teamed up with a burglar?"

"But he said he needs money, Jupe!" Bob reminded him excitedly. "He's trying to get enough money to go to India, remember?"

"Hey, maybe Elmquist is the burglar himself!" added Pete.

"You forget. Elmquist was asleep in his apartment when the police chased the burglar through the courtyard," said Jupe. "And then he was standing in front of the church with us while the police searched the building—and presumably the burglar was inside posing as a saint."

"But Elmquist seems able to be in two places at once," said Bob. "If he can haunt Mr Prentice's apartment while he's at home downstairs, then he can be inside and outside the church at the same time, too!"

Jupe shook his head in frustration. "It's just not possible. But I agree with you on one thing. There's a lot about Sonny Elmquist that hasn't been explained. I think we should keep an eye on that man, and I have an idea how to do it. I've been working on—"

The telephone on the desk rang. Jupe picked it up. "Yes?" he said. Then, "Oh, Mr Prentice, just a moment."

Jupiter held the telephone receiver near a special microphone and loudspeaker he had rigged up from parts of an old radio. Now all three of the boys could hear what the art collector was saying.

"Please go ahead, Mr Prentice," said Jupiter.

"I have just received a telephone call." The man's voice was shaky and excited. "It was from the person who now has possession of the Carpathian Hound. You told me that it would be a difficult thing to dispose of. Well, he has found the perfect place to sell it. He offers it to me for ten thousand dollars!"

10

A Case of Poison

THE THREE INVESTIGATORS sat in stunned silence.

"Jupiter? Are you there?" Fenton Prentice demanded.

"Uh, yes. Yes, sir." It was not often that Jupiter Jones was taken by surprise, but the old gentleman's announcement had floored him.

"I . . . I do not like the idea of doing business with a criminal," continued Prentice, "but I must have the Hound. It is mine, and if I do not recover it, it may be lost forever. I intend to pay the ransom. I have two days to gather the money."

"Have you notified the police?"

"I do not intend to. I refuse to risk scaring the burglar. I might never get the Hound back."

"I think you should reconsider," said Jupe. "You're dealing with a violent criminal. Don't forget what he did to Earl."

"Precisely. The thief became scared and struck him. I do not wish to give him any reason to fear me. Now, when are you boys returning? I confess, I don't like waiting here alone."

"Has the shadow reappeared?"

"No, but just knowing that he might is . . . unnerving."

"I think we should be able to make the three o'clock bus," said Jupe, looking at Bob and Pete for agreement. They nodded. "We'll be there before dark."

Jupe said good-bye and hung up. "Whew! Now we have to save him from the burglar, too! We'd better pack some extra clothes this time," he said. "Prepare to stay at Prentice's for a few days. I'll meet you at the bus stop a little before three."

"What's this idea you had for watching Elmquist?" asked Pete.

"I'll explain it later. I haven't got it all worked out yet."

Bob and Pete left then. Bob decided to put in a few hours at his part-time job at the Rocky Beach library, where he catalogued and shelved books. Pete ran some errands for his mother. Jupe spent the rest of the morning scraping rust off some garden furniture that Aunt Mathilda wanted fixed up for resale. After lunch he got busy in his workshop, repairing some electronic devices. These he finally packed in a carton, which he carried down to the bus stop along with a knapsack full of clean clothes.

"Hey, what's in the box?" asked Bob. "Some new invention?"

"It's a closed-circuit television camera and receiver," said Jupe. "It used to be in a department store."

"Oh, yeah!" said Pete. "They've got them all over the place now. Security people use them to watch for shoplifters."

"Where'd you get that one?" Bob asked.

"The store that owned this system had a fire," Jupe reported. "The cameras and the monitors were damaged and Uncle Titus was able to buy them for almost nothing. I fixed up this set. It wasn't hard."

"So that's how we're going to watch Sonny Elmquist!" said Bob.

"Right. Since Prentice has no windows opening on to the balcony, we can't watch the courtyard unobserved without a device like this. Of course, we could just sit out on the balcony or by the pool, but I don't want Elmquist—or anyone—to know we're watching. There's a big potted plant outside Mr Prentice's door that can conceal the camera. We'll sit inside and watch the monitor screen."

"Great!" said Pete. "It'll be our own TV show!"

An hour later the boys entered the front gate of Prentice's apartment building, to be met by the ever present Mrs Bortz.

"Back again?" she said. She eyed the carton, which Pete was now carrying. "What's that?" she demanded.

"It's a TV set," said Jupe simply. "A late Christmas present for Mr Prentice."

Jupe glanced past the manager. Murphy, the stockbroker, sat beside the pool smoking a cigarette and enjoying the last of the afternoon sun. Every few seconds he knocked ashes into his special ashtray. When he saw the boys he smiled. "You going to be staying with Mr Prentice tonight?" he asked.

"I think so," said Jupe.

"Good." Murphy put out his cigarette. "The old man must get lonesome. It's nice to have company once in a while. My nephew left today to visit friends and I miss him already." Murphy stood up and went into his apartment.

Mr Prentice was waiting for the boys in his doorway. He was delighted with the closed-circuit television camera.

"We'll set it up at dusk," said Jupe, "before the courtyard lights go on. I believe that's around five-thirty?"

Mr Prentice nodded. "The lights go on automatically, shortly after sunset."

At 5.20 Jupe peeked out the balcony door and said, "Quick, fellows, while no one is watching." He directed Bob and Pete to stand at the edge of the balcony, blocking the view from downstairs of the potted rubber tree outside Mr Prentice's apartment. Then he quickly put the small television camera in position. It stood on a low metal tripod, which Jupe inserted in the earth in the pot. He adjusted the lens so that it pointed down into the courtyard.

"The camera is transistorized," said Jupe as the boys re-entered the apartment. "It runs on batteries. It will only send its signals—the image of what it sees—a few feet, but that's all we need."

He closed the apartment door and set the TV

monitor on a bookcase. Then he plugged it in and turned a dial. After a second, the screen flickered faintly.

"Hey, Jupe, I can't make out a thing!" complained Pete.

"Wait until the courtyard lights come on," said Jupe.

A few minutes later the Investigators and Mr Prentice were looking at a clear picture of the courtyard below. As they watched, Sonny Elmquist came out of his apartment and disappeared into the rear passageway. He returned carrying a laundry bag and went back into his apartment.

Next a plump young blonde woman appeared in the foreground of the TV screen. Evidently she had just come in from the front gate.

"That's Miss Chalmers," said Fenton Prentice.

Miss Chalmers was just about to unlock her door when Mrs Bortz appeared behind her. The manager had a package which she handed to the young woman.

"Apparently something was delivered today for Miss Chalmers," said Mr Prentice. "Mrs Bortz always signs for packages that are delivered when tenants aren't home."

"I'm sure she enjoys that," observed Pete.

"Yes," said Prentice. "It gives her a chance to know even more about her tenants."

Mrs Bortz continued to stand there talking to Miss Chalmers, obviously delaying the young woman and obviously interested in the contents of the package.

Miss Chalmers shrugged finally, put her hand-bag on a table near the pool, and sat down to unwrap her parcel.

Alex Hassell came out of his apartment then, and he, too, stopped to watch Miss Chalmers.

"People in this building don't have many secrets, do they?" said Pete.

Mr Prentice clucked with annoyance. "Miss Chalmers should not let that wretched Bortz woman impose on her," he said. "She is much too good-natured."

Miss Chalmers now had the wrappings off her package, and was lifting the lid off a box. The boys saw her smile. She picked something out of the box, popped it into her mouth, then quickly seized another object from the box.

"Chocolates," said Jupiter.

"That woman would not have to swim so much if she could restrain herself in the presence of sweets," said Mr Prentice.

Below, Miss Chalmers offered the candy box to Mrs Bortz, as if just remembering her manners. Then she stopped, suddenly putting her hand to her throat. The box dropped and chocolates bounced out.

"What . . .?" gasped Pete.

Miss Chalmers lurched forward out of the chair in which she had been sitting. She bent double, then fell to the floor of the courtyard and lay there, writhing.

The Three Investigators raced to the door of the apartment and yanked it open.

"Miss Chalmers!" They heard Mrs Bortz's voice, rough with alarm. "What is it?"

"It hurts!" cried Miss Chalmers. "Oh! Oh, it hurts!"

Jupe, Pete, and Bob raced down the stairs. By the time Prentice caught up with them in the courtyard, Jupiter was sniffing at a piece of the chocolate candy that had fallen from the box. Miss Chalmers was crying, and Mr Murphy had come bolting from his apartment to bend over her. Sonny Elmquist was also there, his apartment door standing open.

"What is it?" demanded Mrs Bortz. She seized Jupe's arm and shook it roughly, causing him to crush the chocolate-covered candy in his hand. Jupe put the gooey mess to his nose, sniffed—and looked up in alarm.

"We'd better get an ambulance!" he cried. "There's something in the candy that shouldn't be there! I think she's been poisoned!"

11

The Night Watch

"FORGET THE AMBULANCE!" said Murphy. "I'll take her to the emergency room in my car!"

"I'll go with you," volunteered Mrs Bortz.

"Take the candy, too!" said Jupe. "So it can be analysed!"

Murphy got his car out of the garage, and Pete managed to get Miss Chalmers into the back seat. Mrs Bortz covered her with a blanket. Jupiter thrust the box of candy at Mrs Bortz. A second later Murphy had roared off.

"Poison!" said Mr Prentice. "Poor Miss Chalmers! Who on earth would want to poison her?"

"We can't be sure anyone did, Mr Prentice," Jupiter pointed out. "It's just that the candy had a peculiar odour."

But two hours later, Mr Prentice and the Three Investigators were sure. Murphy and Mrs Bortz returned from the emergency room at Central Hospital looking extremely grim.

"I have never been so insulted in my life!" said Mrs Bortz.

"What happened?" asked Prentice. He and the boys had just finished dinner when they heard Murphy's car return, and they had rushed downstairs.

"The police!" announced Mrs Bortz. "They asked the most rude questions—how long I'd held the chocolates, for instance. The idea!"

"They were only trying to find out what happened," said Murphy. He sounded tired.

"I would *never* poison anyone," said Mrs Bortz. She stomped to her apartment, slammed the door, and locked it.

"What did happen, Murphy?" asked Alex Hassell. He had come from the laundry room.

"There *was* something poisonous in the chocolates," said Murphy. "The lab at the hospital is doing an analysis now, to find out exactly what. Miss Chalmers had her stomach pumped and is now in a private room under observation. The police were called, of course, and they questioned Mrs Bortz about the package. I wish that woman wouldn't take everything so personally. She acted as if they were accusing *her* of sending poisoned chocolates to Gwen. No one accused her of any such thing."

"How were the chocolates delivered?" asked Jupiter.

"They came through the mail. Nothing unusual."

Mrs Bortz's door opened. The manager had gotten control over herself. She came outside and looked at the pool. "I suppose something good comes of everything," she said. "Gwen Chalmers is the only one who uses the pool in this weather. She won't be swimming for a few days at least. I can have the pool drained and cleaned while she's away. It's long past time that it had a proper cleaning."

Murphy opened his mouth as if to say something, then shrugged, lit a cigarette, and went into his own apartment. Hassell left, too.

Mr Prentice looked sourly at Mrs Bortz and headed for the stairs. "Really, that woman has no sensitivity," he muttered to the boys. "Imagine, worrying about the pool at a time like this!"

"Who would try to poison Miss Chalmers?" wondered Prentice again when he and the Investigators were inside his apartment.

"Someone who knew her or her habits," said Jupe. "Someone who knew that the moment she opened the chocolates, she would eat one or two. The real question is, *why* did someone want to poison her?"

No one had an answer. Jupe sat down cross-legged on the floor where he could keep an eye on the television monitor. The courtyard below was empty.

"You live in a very interesting place," said Jupe to Prentice. "We have known you scarcely three days, and in that time we have caught one intruder in your apartment—Mrs Bortz—and I have twice observed another—the shadow. You have been robbed of an irreplaceable work of art and have received a ransom demand for it. Now one of your neighbours has been poisoned."

"Don't forget the janitor in the church next door," prompted Bob. "He got knocked on the head, and then Jupe got locked in the church, where he saw a phantom priest, or somebody."

"It's all too coincidental," said Jupiter. "There must be some connection. But so far, location is the only link. Everything has happened in or near this building."

"Yeah, and everything's happened when Sonny Elmquist has been around," remarked Pete. "Never when he's away at work."

Mr Prentice suddenly looked up in alarm. "Do you think he can hear us? If he *is* the shadow, then he could be in here listening and we wouldn't know it."

Bob got up and went through the apartment room by room, turning on all the lights. No shadow person lurked anywhere. Prentice was reassured by the empty brightness of the apartment and busied himself with the dinner dishes. The Investigators settled down to watch the TV monitor.

For several hours nothing happened in the courtyard, except that Mrs Bortz carried some garbage back to the trash cans. The boys began to get bored and sleepy.

"Look!" said Jupe suddenly. Sonny Elmquist had come out of his apartment and was standing by the pool, staring into the water. The Investigators watched him closely.

The door to Murphy's apartment opened, and the stocky man came out. He was smoking, carrying the ashtray that he usually used. He made a gesture of half-greeting to Elmquist. Then he put his cigarette out, set the ashtray on a table, and went out the front gate. An instant later the boys heard a car start. Pete went to the window that overlooked the street.

"He's going someplace," he reported. "He's going fast."

"Possibly he is simply going for a drive," said Prentice. "He was upset, I think, when he returned from the hospital. Probably he can't sleep."

Sonny Elmquist went back into his apartment and pulled his curtains.

"Blast!" said Pete. "We can't see what he's doing."

"Doubtless he's getting ready to go to work," said Jupe. "He's due at the market at midnight."

Just then the lights in the courtyard below were snapped out. The screen of the television monitor became a grey blue, with the only light visible a patch of brightness behind Elmquist's curtains.

"Double-blast!" said Pete. "Now we can't see anything."

"There's an automatic timer on the lights," said Mr Prentice. "They go out at eleven."

"So much for closed-circuit TV." Jupiter snapped off the set.

"Well, if it's dark, we don't really need it, do we?" said Pete. "Look, if Elmquist is going to work tonight, and if he *is* the one who's been getting in here, he'll have to pull his funny stuff in the next hour or not at all. You guys stay in here with Mr Prentice. I'm going out on the balcony to watch. No one will be able to see me. I'll stay behind that rubber tree."

"Don't ring the doorbell if you see anything," warned Jupe. "Just knock very softly. We'll come out."

"Okay." Pete got into his ski jacket. For a moment the lights in the Prentice apartment were extinguished, and Pete opened the door and stepped out on to the balcony. The door closed behind him, but this time it was not locked. Pete knew that Jupe and Bob were waiting on the other side of the door and would be there, ready, if he needed them.

The lights in Elmquist's apartment glowed for a short time, then went out. Pete waited for Elmquist to come out of the apartment and set off for work. Nothing happened. A faint reflection of the city lights kept the pool area below from being a complete pit of blackness. Pete knew he could see anything that moved down there, but nothing did move.

Soon after midnight a man came in through the front gate. Pete stiffened, then relaxed as the dark figure stopped at a poolside table. It was Murphy, retrieving his ashtray. The stockbroker went into his apartment, and a light went on behind his curtains.

Pete blinked. For a few seconds—for just as long as it had taken Murphy to get his ashtray and open his door—Pete had taken his eyes off Elmquist's door. In those few seconds, Elmquist had come out of his own place. In the faint light from Murphy's windows, Pete could see that Elmquist was dressed in a bathrobe and slippers. The young

97

man moved noiselessly around the pool, approaching Murphy's door.

Pete blinked again. Elmquist was gone! Twenty yards from his own front door, he had vanished!

Pete rapped quickly on Prentice's door. Without waiting for anyone to answer, he stole down the stairs towards the courtyard. He intended to put himself at Elmquist's door, to intercept the wandering young man when he returned.

Pete had just reached the decking that surrounded the pool when his foot came down on something soft and alive!

There was a hideous screeching sound—the sound of a creature in torment!

Shuddering, Pete tried to jump aside, but the living, moving thing had gotten between his ankles. He shouted once and fell forward.

The screech came again.

As if on slow-motion film, Pete saw the edge of the pool come towards him. He saw something clinging to his leg. He felt claws. Then, with a splash, he was in the pool!

Alex Hassell's door flew open.

The courtyard lights snapped on.

Pete came to the surface of the pool, gasping and spitting chlorinated water.

The screeching menace snarled, swam to the edge of the pool, and was scooped out by Hassell. It was a black cat.

"You . . . you brute!" said Hassell to Pete.

Pete clambered out of the pool into the chill air.

"Mr Prentice!" shouted Mrs Bortz. She had

appeared wrapped in her robe, her hair rolled on pink curlers. "Mr Prentice, you will *have* to keep these boys from wandering around in the night!"

Jupiter came down the stairs. Sonny Elmquist was suddenly standing in the door of his apartment.

"I . . . I wasn't able to sleep," said Pete lamely.

Murphy's door opened. "Now what?" bellowed the stockbroker.

"That fresh kid stepped on one of my cats!" said Hassell. He cuddled the dripping, forlorn creature in his arms. "It's okay, baby," he said soothingly. "You come with me. I'll get you all fixed up. Don't pay any attention to that nasty boy!"

"I don't want to catch you out here again!" said Mrs Bortz angrily.

"No, ma'am," said Pete.

Mrs Bortz retreated to her lair and turned off the lights.

"Another night off?" Jupe said, eyeing Elmquist.

Sonny Elmquist nodded.

"Sorry it's not a quieter one," said Jupe.

"I almost . . . almost saw . . ."

"What?" asked Jupe.

"Nothing." Elmquist rubbed his eyes. "I was dreaming, I guess. Not really awake . . ."

The skinny young man stepped back and closed his door.

Pete went up the stairs to Prentice's apartment on the double. Jupe followed him. Prentice was waiting in the living room with a huge towel, and in the bathroom Bob had turned on a hot shower.

"Where'd Elmquist come from?" demanded Pete as he peeled off his jacket. "I was out there watching and I saw him go around the pool towards Murphy's place. Then, all of a sudden, he wasn't there any more. He wasn't anyplace. So I went downstairs to look for him and I stepped on that darned cat and—"

"I saw it," said Jupe. "You fell in the pool. And Elmquist came out of his apartment."

"But that's impossible!" declared Pete. "He wasn't *in* his apartment when I fell in the pool. There was no way he could be in his apartment. He was over by Murphy's, and then he wasn't anywhere!"

12

Crack-up!

FOR THE REST OF THE NIGHT, Bob and Jupe took turns watching from the balcony. There was no further movement in the courtyard until four, when Mrs Bortz came out of her apartment. She was wearing a heavy tweed coat. Jupe saw her and dodged into Prentice's apartment.

"Mrs Bortz is going out," Jupe reported to Prentice. The old gentleman had not gone to bed at all. He had spent the night sitting up, propped against a corner of the sofa, dozing now and then.

"Of course," said Prentice when he heard this.

"At four a.m.?" questioned Jupiter.

Prentice yawned. "The market is open twenty-four hours a day," Prentice reminded Jupe. "Mrs Bortz always does her marketing on Thursdays and she always leaves at four."

Jupe could only stare at Prentice.

"She claims the market isn't crowded at this hour," said Prentice. "It is my opinion, however, that at this hour she can be reasonably sure nothing will be happening here, so she won't miss anything if she's away. Mr Murphy will not leave for his office until five o'clock. The other tenants are always in bed at this time."

Bob and Pete came in from the den, where they had been napping. "You mean she's so nosy she can't stand to be away from here unless everybody's asleep?" said Pete.

"It is strange, compulsive behaviour," said Prentice. "She's like a spider who cannot leave her web. Her only interest is in the people who live here; she watches them constantly. That is her existence."

Bob went to the front window and pulled aside the curtains. He heard a car start and saw the red glow of tail lights on the cement below. Then a grey sedan began to back out from under the building.

"I'm surprised her battery doesn't go dead, if she only uses the car once a week," said Bob.

"She has to summon the men from the garage fairly often," said Prentice.

The sedan backed into the street, turned, and started forward slowly.

Then, in the pre-dawn stillness, the boys and Prentice heard an explosion and a scream.

Prentice jumped up from the sofa.

Jupiter leaped to the window.

A little way down the street, the sedan swerved first to the left and then to the right. Smoke billowed out from under the hood.

Mrs Bortz screamed again. The car, now completely out of control, smashed into the kerb, blowing both front tyres. With a horrible crunch, it struck a hydrant head on.

Mrs Bortz screamed again and again. The

hydrant had snapped off level with the ground, and water spurted up around the car.

"Call the fire brigade!" shouted Pete to Prentice.

Bob ran towards the doors. "We'd better get her out of there before she drowns," he said.

The boys reached the courtyard just as Murphy, clad in a bathrobe, and Elmquist, who had thrown a coat on over his pyjamas, were going out through the front gate.

"Mrs Bortz!" shouted Murphy. The big man ran towards the wrecked car.

The boys passed Elmquist and overtook Murphy. They waded through ice-cold water and then groped through the bone-chilling cascade from the broken hydrant to reach the door of the sedan.

Mrs Bortz sat rigidly behind the wheel, staring straight ahead and screaming—screaming as if she would never stop.

"Mrs Bortz!" Jupe pulled at the door handle. The car door was locked.

Murphy beat at the window next to Mrs Bortz. The woman turned, stunned, and stared at him.

"Open the door!" yelled Murphy.

She fumbled with the button on the door. A second later Murphy had yanked the door open. He and Bob dragged the hysterical woman out of the car.

There were sirens on the street then, and an emergency truck from the fire brigade pulled up. Men in black raincoats swarmed down. One took a look at the situation and turned to say a few words to the driver of the truck. The man put his vehicle in gear and sped off towards the corner.

A moment later, the fire hydrant stopped spouting. Murphy, Elmquist, Bob, and Jupe stood with Mrs Bortz, who was speechless from shock.

" How'd you do that ?" said Murphy to a fireman.

"There's a master valve at the corner," said the fireman. He looked at Mrs Bortz. "Were you driving ?" he asked.

She didn't answer.

"We'd better get her inside," said Murphy. "She'll catch pneumonia standing out here."

Bob and Jupe almost had to drag Mrs Bortz up the steps into the building. Murphy got her keys from the car to open her door. The fireman had come to the door and stood there. A policeman appeared behind him.

"Who hit the hydrant ?" the policeman said.

Mrs Bortz stood in her living room. "Someone shot at me," she said. She seemed to speak without moving her lips.

"You'd better get out of your wet things, ma'am," said the policeman quietly. "Then, if you're feeling okay, maybe you'd like to tell us about it."

She nodded and disappeared into a hallway.

Jupe realized that his own teeth were chattering. "I'm going to change, too," he told the officer.

"You see anything ?" asked the policeman.

"I saw the car start up the street," said Jupe.

"Okay, go and change your clothes, then come

back here." He turned to Bob and Pete. "You, too."

A few minutes later the boys returned in dry clothes and gave their report to the police.

A breakdown truck had arrived on the street. Several men in police uniforms and one man in plain clothes were clustered around the wrecked car.

"If anybody shot at her, he missed," said the plain-clothes man.

"There *was* a shot," said Jupe. "I heard it. Just as she started to drive down the street, there was a shot or . . . or an explosion."

The sedan, listing to one side atop the broken hydrant, was brilliantly lit by the headlamps of the breakdown truck.

"No bullet holes," said the plain-clothes man.

Jupe spotted something on the ground—some bit of reddish paper, sodden now with water. He bent and picked it up, peering closely at it.

"A cloud of black smoke," he said.

"What?" asked the plain-clothes man.

"Just after the shot, or the explosion, a cloud of smoke came out from under the hood of the car."

The plain-clothes man went to the front of the car and opened the bonnet.

A uniformed officer shone a torch on the motor.

There were bits of paper and what appeared to be singed cotton wadding strewn over the engine block. The radiator hoses were scorched and the fan belt had snapped.

"Not a shot," decided the plain-clothes man. "An explosive device. There was some kind of a bomb under the bonnet!"

He banged the bonnet down. "Take it away!" he shouted to the driver of the breakdown truck. "Take it to the police garage!"

He turned to the boys. Murphy had joined them again, and Sonny Elmquist was hunched near the stairway to the building. Alex Hassell had come out, looking as if his slacks had been put on over his pyjamas.

"Somebody was out to get her!" said Hassell.

"She have any enemies?" asked the policeman.

"A whole building full of them," said Murphy sourly, "though I can't imagine anybody planting a bomb in her car."

The stockbroker yawned. "My name's Murphy," he told the plain-clothes man. "Just for the record. John Murphy. I live in 1E and I didn't see anything. I only heard the explosion and the car smashing up. I ran out with these kids and helped get the old bat out of her car. Now, since we haven't had much sleep, I'm going to declare a day off and go back to bed. If you want to ask me any questions, feel free, but don't do it before noon. I plan to sleep till then."

The stockbroker plodded away up the stairs.

The policeman looked after him. "Things have been really weird on this block the last couple of days," he remarked.

"You said it!" agreed Pete. He squinted towards the east, where a pink glow was beginning to light the sky. "If there's anything to the law of averages, we ought to have a quiet morning. What else can happen?"

13

Fire!

AFTER THE NIGHT'S EXCITEMENT, Mr Prentice and the exhausted Investigators fell sound asleep. Late in the morning Prentice served an excellent breakfast to the boys. Jupe turned on the TV monitor but only glanced at it occasionally. The apartment building was very quiet.

"I have to go to the bank," announced Prentice. "By tomorrow I must have ten thousand in cash in small bills. I would be most pleased if one of you young men would accompany me."

"Certainly, Mr Prentice," said Jupe. "However, I think you should inform the police of what you are doing."

"No," said Prentice. "The Carpathian Hound is too precious to risk losing. If the thief feels he is in danger, he might simply destroy it. We must follow his instructions to the letter."

Jupiter went to the window. There was a taxi on the street below. The driver came down the steps from the building carrying a suitcase. Mrs Bortz followed him.

"Mrs Bortz is leaving," announced Jupiter as the cab drove away.

"She has a sister in Santa Monica," said Prentice.

"She goes to her when she's ill or in trouble."

"I guess she *is* in trouble," said Pete. "Having a bomb planted in your car is—"

He was interrupted by the sound of smashing glass which could be heard even through the closed door to the balcony.

"Fire!" shouted someone. "Help! Fire!"

Instantly the group in Prentice's apartment was out the door.

On the courtyard level there were flames blazing on the curtains in John Murphy's windows. Sonny Elmquist, in bare feet and with his hair standing on end, was smashing through the windows with an iron pool chair.

"My stars!" cried Mr Prentice. He dashed back inside to call the fire brigade.

Pete was down the stairs and snatching up a second chair before Jupe and Bob even made it to the courtyard.

Alex Hassell came stumbling from his apartment.

"Mr Murphy!" yelled Pete.

He brushed away bits of broken glass from the window sill and swatted at the flaming curtains.

"Here!" Jupe had spotted a fire extinguisher in a niche near the stairway. He grabbed it and ran towards the blaze.

In an instant, spray from the extinguisher leaped to smother the fire in the curtains. The flames died with a resentful hiss, and the boys and Elmquist clambered in through the window. Jupe aimed the fire extinguisher at a smouldering sofa which stood next to the window, and squirted the Christmas tree beyond the sofa for good measure.

The boys choked in the smoke-filled apartment. They shouted, but Murphy did not answer. Jupe and Pete crouched low to avoid the worst of the fumes and crept forward. They found Murphy collapsed in the doorway between the living room and the bedroom.

"We've got to get him out, quick!" gasped Pete. He seized Murphy by an arm, turned him over, and slapped at his face.

Murphy didn't stir.

"Drag him," ordered Jupe.

Jupe took one arm and Pete the other. Bob ran over and grabbed the man's feet. Behind them, Sonny Elmquist choked and sputtered.

"Get out of here!" warned Pete. "You want to keel over, too?"

Elmquist got to the door and unlocked it.

Still crouching, the Investigators hauled the unconscious man towards the doorway, to the light and the fresh air.

Murphy was dead weight, as heavy as a sack of coal. The boys managed, though, and did it quickly. In seconds they had the stockbroker beside the pool, stretched out with the sun glaring down on to his pale face.

"Oh, dear!" said Mr Prentice.

Alex Hassell stared. "Is he . . . is he . . . ?"

Pete had his ear to Murphy's chest. "He's alive."

The firemen arrived then, with oxygen and an ambulance. They surged into Murphy's apartment to put out the last smouldering sparks in the curtains and the upholstery.

The fire captain came within a few minutes and joined his men inside the apartment.

One of the ambulance men took the oxygen mask away from Murphy's face when the stock-broker gasped, opened his eyes, and pushed at the thing with one hand.

"Okay, mister," said the ambulance driver. "You got a dose of smoke, that's all."

Murphy tried to sit up.

"Take it easy," said the ambulance man. "We'll get you to the emergency room."

Murphy looked as if he might protest, then sank back on to the flagstones.

"George, bring the stretcher," said the ambulance driver to his partner.

Murphy lay quietly and allowed himself to be lifted on to the stretcher. The two ambulance men covered him with a grey blanket and started to take him away.

"Hadn't someone better go with him?" said Hassell.

"My nephew," said Murphy weakly. "I'll send for my nephew."

A moment later the ambulance left, its siren screaming.

The fire captain appeared in the doorway of the Murphy apartment. "Same old story," he said. He held out a half-burned cigarette which was wet with foam from the fire extinguisher. "Fell asleep with a cigarette going. Cigarette dropped into the sofa, smouldered there, and then set the thing on fire. That started the curtains burning, and . . ."

"Lucky I saw it." Sonny Elmquist was still in his bare feet. He was very pale.

"Lucky for the guy who lives here. He might have been killed. You caught it just in time. That Christmas tree in there is a real tree. If the flames had reached it, the whole place would have gone up in a minute."

"He went to sleep with a cigarette?" said Jupiter.

"Lots of people do, son," said the fire captain.

"But he had that special ashtray," said Jupe. "He claimed it was foolproof—that he could leave a cigarette in it and not worry. The cigarette couldn't fall out."

"Anything can happen if a guy lights up while he's sleepy," advised the fire captain.

"And Mr Murphy *was* sleepy," pointed out Mr Prentice. "He said he was going to sleep until noon. He must have thrown himself down on the sofa and dropped off."

"But we found him on the floor headed for the bedroom. If he was sleeping on the sofa, why didn't he just open the front door and walk out?" asked Jupiter.

"He got confused in the smoke," said the fireman soothingly. "It's the easiest thing to do. By the time the smoke reached him, he wouldn't know which way was which."

Jupiter and the others retreated from the firemen, who were pulling the sofa apart to make sure no trace of fire remained.

"That'll be a fine mess to clean up," said Hassell.

"Mrs Bortz will have a fit when she sees it." Sonny Elmquist looked pleased. "Say, where *is* Mrs Bortz?"

"She left in a cab a little while ago," said Bob.

"Where will the emergency ambulance take Mr Murphy?" Jupe asked the fire captain.

"The receiving room at Central Hospital. That's the emergency hospital for this area. If they decide he can't be released, he'll stay there—or be moved to another hospital, if that's what he wants."

Jupiter nodded. "Central Hospital," he repeated. "That's where Miss Chalmers is. But . . . *why* is Murphy going there?"

"It's the emergency hospital," said the fireman.

"That's not what I mean," said Jupe, "Mr Murphy was very careful with cigarettes. He shouldn't have had a fire. It just doesn't make sense!"

14

The Wanderers

"THERE'S A JINX ON THIS HOUSE!" declared Alex Hassell after the firemen had departed. "First Gwen Chalmers, then Mrs Bortz, and now Murphy!"

"It all began with the burglary," said Mr Prentice. He did not look at Sonny Elmquist, who was slouched on a lounge, his eyes half-closed against the sunlight. "Things were quite peaceful until three nights ago, when the burglar ran through this courtyard. Since then, nothing has been the same."

Jupe nodded. "There is one obvious conclusion," he said. "The Carpathian Hound is here! And the person who stole the Carpathian Hound is most likely here, too!"

"Young man, what are you talking about?" demanded Hassell. "There isn't any dog here, stolen or otherwise. My cats would know if there was a dog here!"

"It's a crystal statue of a dog," explained Fenton Prentice. "I commissioned the Hound from the artist Edward Niedland, and loaned it to him for his show at the Maller Gallery. It was stolen from Edward's home on Monday night."

Alex Hassell gave a short, mocking laugh. "So that's what Mrs Bortz meant! She told me you were going to get a dog, and that I'd better watch out for my cats. A glass dog! Hah!"

Prentice sighed. "She'd been reading my papers. I'm sure she thought I was getting a real dog. So she blabbed it all over the building—and then someone stole the Hound!"

"Well, I didn't!" snapped Hassell. "What's more, I'm not going to stay here while somebody's poisoning people and blowing up cars. I'm going to a motel!"

He hurried to his apartment. In a short time he was out again with a pet carrier in one hand and a suitcase in another. "I'll be back at five to feed my kitties," he announced. "Naturally I'm taking Tabitha with me. If you want to reach me, I'll be at the Ramona Inn until sanity sets in around here."

Hassell glared at Mr Prentice. "You can search my apartment if you wish," he said, "but you'd better have a warrant."

He stalked out. A moment later a car started out front.

"You can search my apartment if you want to," offered Sonny Elmquist. "I've got to go to work at noon, but there's time before then. You don't need a warrant."

"At noon?" said Bob. "I thought you worked nights."

"Doing the early shift today," explained Elmquist. "One of the other guys called in sick."

"I'm sure the Hound isn't in your apartment," said Jupiter quietly. "It isn't in any apartment in this building."

Sonny Elmquist looked slightly disappointed. He shrugged and returned to his own place.

"How can you be so sure?" asked Prentice.

"For the obvious reason that Mrs Bortz *is* a snoop," Jupe explained, "and she does her snooping here. She pries into the affairs of the tenants and everyone knows it. Until today, she has not been away from here. She has a pass key and can enter any apartment but yours. If I had stolen the Carpathian Hound and I lived in this building, I wouldn't keep the Hound in *my* apartment."

"Yes. I suppose you're right."

"But that doesn't mean that the Hound isn't close by. Why else would someone be trying to get so many tenants out of the way? Yesterday Miss Chalmers was poisoned. Today Mrs Bortz had her car bombed—and narrowly escaped injury. Then there was a fire in Mr Murphy's apartment. I wonder about that. I'd like to talk to Murphy. When he's feeling better he may remember something."

Bob frowned. "You think the fire wasn't an accident?"

"It's possible."

"Hey, do you suppose Sonny Elmquist set it? He came to the rescue awfully quick. Maybe he walked through the walls first, to light the fire, and then made a show of rescuing Murphy before the flames went too far!"

"How are you going to prove a crazy theory like that?" asked Pete.

"For a start," said Bob decisively, "I'm going to talk to Dr Barrister." He was referring to a professor of anthropology at nearby Ruxton University—a man who had helped the Three Investigators before with his knowledge of witchcraft and the occult. "Maybe Elmquist didn't set the fire, but he sure seems able to walk through walls. Dr Barrister may know of an explanation."

"Well, I'm going to stick to the real world!" said Pete. "I think I'll tail Elmquist when he goes to work. He says he's going to the market, but we only have his word for it. I can also make sure that Hassell does check into that motel."

"And I," announced Jupiter, "am going to pay a few hospital calls. I need some information from Miss Chalmers and Mr Murphy."

Mr Prentice looked alarmed. "I say! I had planned to go to the bank with you boys. I don't want to carry all that ransom money by myself."

"No, and you shouldn't stay here alone," said Jupe. "Do you have a friend who could keep you company?"

"Charles Niedland, of course!"

Prentice immediately called Niedland, who promised to be at Paseo Place in a few minutes.

Bob phoned Dr Barrister and then hopped in a Twenty minutes later he was in the pro-ffice at Ruxton University. The man's l face was bright with excitement.

now?" demanded Barrister. "What

sort of mystic phenomena have the Three Investigators uncovered?"

Bob explained about the shadow-person who visited Mr Prentice's apartment.

"Hmm!" Barrister said. "I don't believe this is in my field. I am an expert on the folklore of the Maori tribes and on witchcraft as practised in the Caribbean and other areas. What you describe seems to be a true psychic occurrence. I believe in many things which other people don't take as the truth, but I do not believe in ghosts. However," and here Barrister brightend, "I have a colleague whose mind is open on the subject."

Bob chuckled. "I knew you could help us."

"My pleasure," replied Barrister. "Come along. I'll take you to meet Professor Lantine. She's the head of our parapsychology department. Half the faculty here think she's loony and the other half are afraid she can read their minds. You'll enjoy meeting her."

Professor Lantine, whom they found in a bare little brick building behind the gymnasium, turned out to be a pleasant-looking woman in her forties. She was reading letters when Bob and Dr Barrister came into her office. She looked up at Barrister with a broad smile and waved a piece of paper.

"Guess what?" she said. "This note's from a man in Dubuque who claims he's haunted by the ghost of his sister—but he doesn't have a sister."

"You have the most fascinating mail, Eugenia," said Barrister. He sat down across the desk from

Prof. Lantine and motioned to Bob to take a seat.

"This is Bob Andrews," he said. "He's part of a firm of private investigators, and he has a story which I believe will interest you."

"Private investigators?" echoed Professor Lantine. Her eyes sparkled with amusement. "Aren't you a bit on the young side?"

"Youth has its advantages, you know," said Dr Barrister. "Young people have a lot of energy, a lot of curiosity, and not too many prejudices. Bob, tell Professor Lantine about your latest case."

Bob again related his story of the happenings in Mr Prentice's apartment. This time he also mentioned Jupe's experience with the phantom priest in the church next door.

"Ah, yes!" said Professor Lantine.

"You've heard of the phantom priest?" asked Bob.

"The present pastor called me about him some time ago," said Professor Lantine. "I am often asked to look into matters of this kind. Father McGovern had never seen the ghost, but his housekeeper was in a complete state of nerves about it. The person your friend saw in the church—a thin, white-haired man dressed in clerical clothes—fits the description. The old pastor was a thin, white-haired man. His picture is in the parlour at the parish house. However, upon questioning the housekeeper, I discovered an interesting thing She comes from a small town in Ireland—Dungalway—and the church in

Dungalway is famous. It is said to be haunted by the ghost of a priest who was lost at sea. I spent several nights in St Jude's Church, and I saw nothing. I also talked to many residents of Paseo Place. Although quite a few of the older ones believed in the phantom priest, none had ever seen him. I think Mrs O'Reilly made him up. Without quite realizing it, I believe that she reconstructed him from the tales of her own childhood.

"Your spectral visitor in the apartment is something else again."

Professor Lantine leaned forward. "You say that he has appeared in Mr Prentice's apartment when you knew—as certainly as anyone could know—that he was in his own apartment sound asleep?"

"That's right," Bob confirmed.

Professor Lantine smiled. "Delicious!" she exclaimed. "He's a wanderer!"

"Well, I guess he is," agreed Bob. "But Mr Prentice doesn't think it's delicious. How does Elmquist do it?"

Professor Lantine went to a file cabinet and pulled out several folders. "If he is a true wanderer," she said, "he gets out of his body when he's asleep and walks around."

Bob gaped at her.

She sat down again and opened a file folder. "We don't have many cases that have been examined under laboratory conditions," she said. "People who do this sort of thing don't often come into the laboratory. They keep it to themselves. They decide they're going barmy or they think they have second sight. But a person came into the lab just last year.

"She was an ordinary housewife, living in Montrose. I can't tell you her name because that's confidential."

Bob nodded.

"She'd been troubled for some time," said Professor Lantine. "She dreamed true dreams, you see."

Dr Barrister leaned forward. "You mean, Eugenia, that she dreamed things and then they happened?"

"Not quite. She dreamed, for example, that she was at a birthday party in her mother's house in Akron. She saw everything quite clearly. It was her mother's birthday, and her two sisters were there. There was a birthday cake with white frosting and pink lettering and a single candle. She described the entire dream to her husband the next morning. He didn't pay much attention until she got a letter from one of her sisters. Enclosed with the letter was a photograph of the birthday party. It showed exactly what the housewife had seen in her dream. The family members were wearing the same clothes, and there was even a white cake with pink lettering and one candle. The woman's husband became upset and urged her to come see us

"She confessed that this sort of thing happened to her rather frequently. She didn't like it and she tried not to think about it. But when she dreamed she often saw things that were taking place far away, where she had no way of knowing what was going on, and it would turn out later that she had witnessed a real event."

"You said you tested this under laboratory conditions," said Bob.

"Yes. We persuaded her to stay here at the university for a few days. She slept in a room in the lab where we could observe her through a one-way window. She knew that on a shelf above her bed—a shelf too high for her to reach—was a piece of paper with a number written on it. It was a long number—ten digits—and no one knew what the number was. A secretary in another office had typed it out by hitting keys at random. Without looking at what she'd typed, she'd folded the paper and put it in an envelope.

"After her first night sleeping in the lab, the Montrose housewife didn't know what the number was. But she was able to describe the envelope, which had a blob of blue sealing wax on it. And yet she had never left her bed the whole night.

"We then had a janitor open the envelope, take out the paper without looking at it, and place it face up on the shelf. The housewife slept under the shelf a second night. In the morning, she was able to tell us the number. We got the paper down and checked, and she was absolutely right!"

"You were watching the whole night?" asked Bob. "She never got up and tried to reach the shelf?"

"She never moved the whole night. But somehow, she was able to leave her body and read that number. Or, as we say, her astral body left her physical body."

Bob thought for a second. "But that doesn't prove anything!" he objected.

"It would prove how the wanderer at your client's apartment knows that your client owns a mandala," said Dr Barrister.

"But no one saw that woman move," said Bob. "Our client has actually seen Sonny Elmquist, or someone who looks like him, in his apartment."

"And always while Elmquist is asleep?" said Professor Lantine.

"So far as we know."

"That is rare, but it *has* happened," she declared. "Here's another case, slightly different."

She opened a second file folder. "A man who lives in Orange," she said. "All his life he has had disturbing dreams—dreams of being in places and seeing things that he later learned were true events. Unlike the Montrose woman, however, his astral body had actually been seen!

"The man from Orange had a friend in Hollywood—I'll call him Jones. One night Jones was sitting quietly at home, reading a book. His dog barked, and he thought someone was prowling in his yard. He got up to investigate, and in the entry hall he saw the man who lived in Orange. Jones saw him so clearly that he spoke to him—called him by name. The man didn't answer. Instead he turned and went upstairs. When Jones followed him, no one was there.

"Jones found the affair so upsetting that he immediately called his friend in Orange, who answered the telephone himself. The man had been sound asleep, dreaming of being in Jones' house, of seeing Jones reading, and of having Jones confront him in the hall. In his dream, the man from Orange felt threatened when Jones spoke to him, so he fled up the stairs and hid in a closet. The dream ended when the telephone rang."

"Good grief!" exclaimed Bob.

"Yes," said Professor Lantine. "It is amazing—and frightening. It frightens the people who have the power to wander about this way, and it frightens the people who glimpse the wanderers."

"Sonny Elmquist has scared Mr Prentice, all right!" said Bob. "But how can we be sure that he is a wanderer?"

"You can't," said Professor Lantine. "He might consent to come in for some observed experiments. They might prove he has this strange ability. Then again, they might prove nothing."

"I see," said Bob. "In the meantime, Mr Prentice has no way of keeping him out?"

"If he is truly a wanderer, no. However, Mr Prentice shouldn't be alarmed. These people are harmless. They can't do anything. They're only observers, you see."

"You mean they can't touch anything?"

"At least, they apparently can't move anything," said Professor Lantine. "The Montrose housewife, for example, couldn't read the number in the envelope. We had to open the envelope for her."

"So if Elmquist is a wanderer, he can't do anything while he's roaming around," concluded Bob.

"So far as we know, he can't."

"Sonny Elmquist wants to go to India," said Bob. "He wants to study there."

Professor Lantine nodded. "There is a widespread belief that Indian mystics know secrets that are denied to Westerners," she said. "I doubt it. However, if Mr Elmquist is truly a wanderer, he may think he'll find out more about it in India."

"Well, so much for the shadow in Mr Prentice's apartment," said Bob. "But what about the phantom priest? What about ghosts?"

Professor Lantine shrugged. "I haven't been able to collect one shred of evidence that the phantom priest exists anywhere except in the mind of that housekeeper. Perhaps your friend saw the phantom priest in the church, perhaps not. I've never actually seen a ghost, and I've been a ghost hunter for many years. Maybe they exist. Who can tell?"

15

The Victims

WHEN BOB ANDREWS had departed for Ruxton University, Jupe called Central Hospital. He was told that John Murphy, after being treated for smoke inhalation, had been taken to Belvedere Clinic, where his doctor was on staff. Gwen Chalmers was still in Central. Jupe decided to see her first.

He found Miss Chalmers in a private room. She was sitting up in bed, staring unhappily out the window.

"Hi," she said to Jupe, when he appeared in the doorway. "You're Mr Prentice's young friend, aren't you?"

"Yes," said Jupiter. "How are you feeling?"

"Not bad, considering somebody tried to kill me," she said. "Also I'm hungry. They won't give me anything to eat except gelatin and milk." She kicked impatiently at the bedcovers. "Don't ever get poisoned," she advised Jupe.

"I'll try not to!" he said. He looked carefully at the woman. Although she was upset, her face was not the face of a disagreeable person. There were creases in the corners of her mouth, as if she laughed a lot.

"What was the poison, do you know?" asked Jupiter.

"Some common chemical," said Miss Chalmers. She sounded a little bitter about this. "The police told me the name but it didn't register. It wasn't anything like arsenic or strychnine—you know, those classy poisons used in mystery stories."

"Lucky for you!" said Jupiter. "If you had eaten strychnine, you wouldn't be here now!"

"I know, I know! I should be grateful the stuff only made me sick. Getting poisoned chocolates is dramatic enough." She laughed.

"Were the police able to trace anything?"

"They said the poison can't be traced," answered Gwen Chalmers. "And you can buy that brand of chocolates anywhere."

Her eyes wandered to the potted plant sitting on her locker.

"A gift?" asked Jupe.

Miss Chalmers nodded. "The girls I work with sent that," she said. "I called my office this morning, and the plant was here right away. Nice."

"You get on well with the people, don't you?" said Jupe.

She laughed. "You sound just like the cops! They were around half the morning trying to find out if I have any enemies. What nonsense! People like me don't have enemies."

"I'm sure you don't," said Jupiter. "Mr Prentice will be glad to know you're better."

"He's a nice man," she said. "I like him. I'm

glad he's going to get a dog."

Jupe stood very still. "The Carpathian Hound?"

"Yes. He told me . . ."

"He told you he was getting a Carpathian Hound?"

She frowned as if trying to remember. "No, come to think of it, he didn't tell me. I guess it was Mrs Bortz. Yes, I remember. Last Saturday, I was out by the pool and Mrs Bortz was hanging around pretending to wait for the postman. She said he was getting a dog and he hadn't notified her officially. She was kind of upset about it. She wasn't sure we should have a dog in the building, although I can't see why not. Alex Hassell has all those stray cats coming around all the time."

Jupe nodded. "Well, is there anything I can bring you from home?"

She shook her head. "The ladies' auxiliary have been around with toothbrushes and toothpaste and combs and everything I need," she said. "Anyway, I'll be home tomorrow or the next day. They're just having me stay awhile for observation."

Jupe said good-bye and left, musing.

So Miss Chalmers had known of the Carpathian Hound, although she, too, had completely misunderstood the situation. No doubt everyone in the building knew that Mr Prentice would shortly acquire a dog of some type. But how many people knew the dog was actually a crystal sculpture by the deceased artist, Edward Niedland?

Might Elmquist know? Might Murphy? It

would be interesting to hear what Murphy had to say.

A cab stood in the taxi rank in front of the hospital. The driver was slouched in the front seat reading a newspaper.

"Do you know where Belvedere Clinic is?" asked Jupiter.

"Sure, kid. Down at Wilshire and Yale."

Jupe got into the cab. "I'd like to go there."

"Okay." The driver flipped the flag that started his meter and drove away from Central. Jupe realized that they were headed back in the direction of the Prentice apartment. Indeed, Belvedere Clinic turned out to be a small private hospital only two blocks from Paseo Place.

Jupe paid the driver and went into the building.

Compared to Central Hospital, it was elegant. The reception room was thickly carpeted and tastefully decorated with some Christmas ornaments. The receptionist was dressed not in white, but in a soft pink smock. She called John Murphy's room and announced that Jupiter Jones was in the hospital and would like to see Murphy. She then smiled, and gave Murphy's room number to Jupe.

Murphy's room was a big one in a corner. Sunlight streamed through two windows. Murphy was in bed, his usually ruddy face as white as the pillow. His nephew, Harley Johnson, sat in an armchair at the foot of the bed, looking at Murphy with a mixture of amusement and disapproval.

Murphy almost glared at Jupe when he appeared in the room. "If you've come to lecture, too," he snapped, "please don't. I've had all I can take from Harley for one day."

"I always said smoking would kill you," declared Harley. "I didn't expect it would be so soon!"

"I was tired," said Murphy. His voice was sulky. "I was tired, that's all. I'm usually very careful. I don't even keep cigarettes in the bedroom."

"Then you should sleep in the bedroom and not on the sofa," said Harley.

Murphy groaned. "There is nothing more terrible than a righteous nephew."

"Is that what happened?" asked Jupiter. "You fell asleep on the sofa and dropped a cigarette?"

"I suppose so," admitted Murphy. "I can't think what else might have happened. I remember coming in—after Mrs Bortz's car exploded—and sitting down. I was going to have one last cigarette and go to bed. I must have dropped off. The next thing I knew the room was full of smoke. I tried to find the door. Then I passed out."

"You went in the wrong direction," said Jupe. "You headed for the bedroom."

Murphy nodded. "You got me out," he said.

"We all did," Jupe told him. "Bob and Pete and Sonny Elmquist. He was the one who saw the fire."

"Creepy little guy," muttered Murphy. "Never liked him much. Now I owe my life to him."

"Mr Murphy," said Jupiter, "did you know about the dog Mr Prentice was going to get?"

"Dog?" Murphy raised his head from his pillow. "Now, what would Prentice do with a dog? I understand he's got an apartment loaded with antiques. A dog? You must be kidding!"

"Mrs Bortz was rather upset about it," said Jupiter.

"She upsets easily. Anyway, who listens to Mrs Bortz? Her tongue's tied in the middle and wags at both ends."

He stretched out as if very weary. "I may move," he said. He looked at Jupe. "You kids ought to get out of that building, too. Place isn't safe."

Harley stood up and came to the foot of the bed. "Don't worry about it now," he advised. "The doctor said you need rest. I'll go around to your place and get things back in shape for you. When you're feeling better, we can look for a new apartment."

Murphy smiled. "You're a good kid, Harley. Sometimes I think you've been a better guardian to me than I've been to you."

Harley and Jupiter left together.

"My uncle smokes too much," said Harley. "He also works too hard and he worries a lot. In a way, I'm almost glad that fire happened."

Jupe shot a look at the young man.

"I don't mean I'm glad he's in the hospital or anything like that," said Harley quickly. "But he's been very nervous lately, and he doesn't sleep well. I noticed that when I was with him over

Christmas. He got up a couple of times and paced around when he thought I was asleep. I'm not sure his business is going well. The smoke inhalation wasn't much. You guys got him out in time. But his doctor wants to keep him in bed for a couple of days and run some tests and just make sure he gets some sleep."

"I'm sure he can use it," said Jupe as they left the clinic and headed down Wilshire to Paseo Place. "Things have been pretty wild in that apartment house recently. You weren't there the night of the burglary, were you?"

"You mean when the burglar ran through the courtyard from the next street? No, I missed it. I was out having an early dinner with friends before catching a show. Uncle John told me about it afterwards. And now I hear that there was a poisoning and a bombing, too. Uncle John's right. The place isn't safe any more."

"Did anyone tell *you* that Mr Prentice was getting a dog?" queried Jupe.

"Nope. But nobody would except my uncle. I mean, I don't hang around in the courtyard when I visit him. I can't stand listening to Mrs Bortz."

Harley whistled when he saw his uncle's windows. A few shards of glass still protruded from the frames, and the burned curtains hung in tatters.

"Guess I'd better call the glazier first," he said as he pulled a set of keys out of his pocket. "I'll bet the inside is a mess, too. I sure picked the wrong time to leave my uncle." He squared his shoulders and disappeared into Murphy's apartment.

Jupe paused a moment before going upstairs, trying to sort out everything in his mind. Was Gwen Chalmers truly an innocent victim? Was Murphy really ignorant of the Carpathian Hound? Was Harley the innocent bystander he seemed to be?

If so, then Sonny Elmquist was the only person unaccounted for. Elmquist was the only neighbour left who might know of the crystal dog. And Elmquist was the only neighbour remaining in the apartment house.

Then Jupe thought of something else. Someone was using violence to get people out of the building. Would the Three Investigators be next?

16

The Invisible Dog

WHEN JUPITER RANG Mr Prentice's doorbell, Charles Niedland opened the door. "Come on in," he invited. "Your friend Bob just got back from Ruxton, and he's bursting to tell us something."

Bob was sitting on the sofa, his notebook open in front of him. Mr Prentice perched on a small antique chair.

"How is Miss Chalmers?" he asked.

"She'll be fine," Jupe reported.

"Thank goodness," said Prentice. "And Mr Murphy? Did you see him?"

"I did. He wasn't badly injured. Did you get the money to ransom the Hound?"

Charles Niedland pointed to a brown paper grocery sack on a lamp table. "I have seldom been so nervous in my life," he said. "I usually carry about three dollars in my wallet and a few credit cards. Fenton Prentice wanders around the city with ten thousand in small bills in a grocery sack!"

Jupe looked at the sack and smiled. "Very clever," he said. "It looks so unimportant, it's practically invisible."

The doorbell rang again and Charles Niedland admitted Pete.

"The market manager doesn't like kids who come in and stand around and read magazines and don't buy anything," he reported. "He told me to beat it. I bought a copy of *Los Angeles Magazine*, but he still told me to scram."

Pete threw himself down on the sofa beside Bob. "Doesn't matter, I suppose," he said. "We know that Sonny Elmquist is at the market right now. And Hassell did check into that motel."

Bob hunched forward. "Good. Then let's talk about Sonny Elmquist."

"What did you find out?" asked Jupiter.

"That some people *can* be in two places at the same time!" said Bob. He went on to relate all that he'd learned at Ruxton about wanderers and astral bodies.

"In other words," said Jupe when Bob had finished, "Elmquist possibly *can* walk through walls or ignore locked doors."

"I guess he can transport himself wherever he wants to be—and maybe to some places he doesn't even *know* he wants to be. How much control he has over it, I don't know. We can't even be sure that he *does* it. But if he's like the wanderers Dr Lantine talked to, he can only do it when he's sleeping."

"Swell!" said Pete briskly. "So today we know he can't be watching. He isn't going to have any chance to doze off. The market manager will see to that!"

Fenton Prentice got up and put the grocery sack in a little cabinet, which he locked.

"I trust he won't decide to stick his astral head through that door," said Prentice.

"Even if he does, he won't see anything but a paper sack," Bob reported. "According to Dr Lantine, the wanderers who go roaming around in their sleep can't really move anything."

"That would explain why nothing has been disturbed since I took the door key away from Mrs Bortz," said Prentice. "It was she who opened drawers and moved things around."

"Yes," said Jupe, "and it explains how Sonny Elmquist knows about your mandala. He could also know about the Carpathian Hound. He could have heard you talk to Mr Niedland on the telephone. But if his astral body can't move anything, he can't be the burglar. He was asleep when the burglary happened."

Jupe scowled and pulled at his lip.

"It's hard to believe," he said, "but it is the only explanation that fits. Unless there are two people in this building who look exactly alike, Elmquist must be a wanderer. And I don't think two identical people could exist in the same building for a period of months without someone realizing it."

"Not with Mrs Bortz here," said Prentice.

Pete, who had moved to the window, reported that Murphy's nephew was leaving the building.

"Then we're alone here." Jupe stared at the cabinet where Prentice had concealed the ransom money. "A sack filled with cash," he said. "Because it's in the sack, the cash is invisible." He began to smile, and suddenly his eyes sparkled.

"Hey, what is it, Jupe?" asked Bob, recognizing the signs of a mental breakthrough.

"Shall I tell you a story?" he replied.

"Oh, c'mon, Jupe!" groaned Pete. "Skip the build-up!"

"It's a tale of murder," said Jupiter, ignoring him. "A piece of fiction I read a long time ago. It's about a murder that was committed with an invisible weapon."

"Yes?" said Fenton Prentice.

"In the story," said Jupe, "a man and his wife were having dinner with a friend in a closed room. The husband and the friend argued during the course of the meal, and the argument quickly became a raging quarrel. The men struggled, and the candles—which were the only light in the room—were knocked over. The wife then heard her husband cry out, and she felt something pull at her skirt. She screamed, and the servants came running. They found the husband dead, and the wife with blood on her skirt. The husband had been stabbed—but there was no weapon in the room. The servants searched and the authorities searched, but no one could find the weapon. At first they concluded that the husband had been killed by a demon."

"How handy to live in an age when one could conclude a thing like that," said Charles Niedland.

"The truth was," said Jupiter, "that he had been killed by an invisible weapon—a knife made of glass. The murderer—the friend who had dined with the couple—had stabbed the husband in the dark and wiped the glass knife off on the wife's skirt. He then put the knife into a pitcher of water that stood on the sideboard. It couldn't be seen in the water.

"Mr Prentice, why would anyone poison Miss Chalmers?" asked Jupe. "Is there any reason, besides the fact that she swam in the pool every night?"

"Good heavens!" said Charles Niedland.

"And Mrs Bortz," Jupe went on. "Certainly she's a snoop, but no one tried to do her any harm —until she said she'd have the pool drained and cleaned. Mr Prentice, we have been looking for a crystal dog which is invisible because it is out in plain sight—just like that glass knife in the water pitcher."

"The pool!" cried Bob. "It's in the pool."

Jupiter stood gleefully with his hands on his hips. "Tomorrow you are to ransom the crystal dog. Suppose we retrieve the dog today? It's the perfect time. There's no one but us in the building."

"My word!" exclaimed Prentice.

Jupe grinned. "Bob," he said, "you go and stand at the back gate and make sure no one comes in that way. Pete, you watch the street from the front gate."

"And what are you going to do?" said Pete.

Jupe was headed out to the balcony, already unbuttoning his shirt. "I'm going swimming."

Bob and Pete went to their posts, and Prentice and Niedland followed Jupe to the pool. He shed all of his clothes but his shorts and, shivering, slid carefully into the shallow end.

"Steady now," said Prentice anxiously.

Jupe waded towards the deep end, scanning the blue and gold tiles on the bottom. When the water reached his chin he ducked under and let himself sink. Then, kicking out like a frog, he propelled himself forward just above the floor of the pool.

He kicked out again, and then he reached for something.

"He's found it!" Fenton Prentice's voice was an excited whisper. "By jove, he's found it!"

Jupe shot to the surface. In his hand he held an object from which a string dangled. He paddled to the edge of the pool and offered his prize up to Fenton Prentice.

"The Hound!" exclaimed the old gentleman. He took the sculpture and turned it over and over in his hands. It was a strangely beautiful figure of a heavily muscled dog with a square massive head. The wide round eyes were rimmed with gold, and gold froth flecked the crystal jowls. The sculpture was about six inches tall, from the bottom of the glass base to the tips of the dog's ears. Between the feet of the animal was a human skull. Someone had tied a long piece of gilt cord around the dog's middle.

"So simple," said Jupiter. "The burglar didn't even have to get into the pool. He lowered the Hound by that cord until it touched bottom, then let go. The gold cord was invisible against the random pattern of blue and gold tiles.

"Ingenious!" said Charles Niedland.

"May I have it back?" said Jupiter to Fenton Prentice.

"What?" said Prentice.

"I said, may I have it? I want to put it back in the pool."

"Why on earth?"

"Because tonight the burglar may come back for the dog. He's still expecting you to deliver the ransom tomorrow. We'll return the invisible dog to its hiding place, and then we'll watch the TV monitor—and find out who the burglar is!"

"I see." But Fenton Prentice still held on to the dog.

"It makes sense, Fenton," said Charles Niedland.

"But . . . but the dog could be injured, chipped, broken!"

"So far the burglar has been careful with it," said Jupe. "I think he'll stay careful."

Fenton Prentice sighed and handed the crystal statue back to Jupe, who lowered it slowly into the water where he'd found it.

"I need a towel," he said. "I don't want anybody to know I've been in the pool. There mustn't be any wet footprints on the deck."

Charles Niedland bounded up the stairs and was back in a minute with several towels and a thick bath mat. Jupe climbed out of the pool on to the mat and hastily dried himself.

"Hassell's coming!" Pete had darted in from the front gate.

"Get Bob!" ordered Jupe as he scooped up his

clothes. "Quick! Everybody upstairs."

As the group dashed into Prentice's apartment, footsteps could be heard on the stairs that led from the street to the gate. Jupe flicked on the TV monitor and watched Alex Hassell stalk stiffly across the court and go into his own apartment.

"He didn't even look at the pool," said Jupe.

"Why should he?" asked Bob.

"Because, even though I was very careful, the water is slightly disturbed. It always is when someone goes into a swimming pool. It won't be completely still again for some time."

"Then Hassell isn't our burglar," decided Pete.

"Either he isn't our burglar, or he's afraid he's being watched. He might notice the pool and be too smart to react visibly. We'll see."

In the courtyard, cats began drifting in. They gathered in a silent semicircle around Alex Hassell's door and sat, waiting. Presently Hassell came out with some dishes. The cats ate as he watched. He petted them and talked to them; then they departed. In a short time Hassell himself left the building.

The boys helped Fenton Prentice cook dinner and they all ate, with one of the Investigators constantly watching the TV monitor. At eleven, the lights in the courtyard went out.

Pete got his jacket out of the closet. "Here we go again with the night watch on the balcony."

"I think I'll watch with you," said Jupe.

Bob stood up. "Count me in, too. Tonight something should happen—and I want to see it!"

17

The Shadow Acts

AT MIDNIGHT, the gate clicked open. The slim, slouching shape of Sonny Elmquist appeared below and went into his apartment. A light shone out briefly from Elmquist's windows and then went out.

The watchers on the balcony waited.

A door opened and closed. The Three Investigators could see someone moving below them!

Pete gripped Jupe's arm.

The shadowy shape drifted slowly to the shallow end of the pool. It slid into the water silently and moved forward, barely making ripples.

Suddenly the Three Investigators heard the person take an audible breath. He dived under the surface with a small splash. Then a beam of light shone under water. Whoever had gone into the pool had a waterproof flashlight. Its beam swept back and forth across the bottom of the pool.

A hand appeared in the beam of light. It stretched down and closed around an invisible object—the transparent Carpathian Hound!

The person surfaced and climbed out of the pool. A moment later a door opened and closed again.

Pete reached back and rapped softly on Prentice's door. It opened immediately.

"It was Elmquist!" whispered Pete.

The Three Investigators, backed up by Prentice and Charles Niedland, hurried down the stairs.

Sonny Elmquist's windows remained dark.

"He could have been wandering in his sleep again," said Pete quietly.

"Nonsense!" declared Jupiter. He rang Elmquist's bell, waited a second, and then rang it again.

"Elmquist!" he shouted. "Elmquist, open the door! Open it, or I'll call the police and they'll break it down."

The door opened. Elmquist stood there wrapped in a bathrobe, his bare feet and legs showing beneath the robe.

"What?" he said. "I was sleeping. What is it?"

Jupe reached in around the doorway and flipped on an electric switch. A lamp went on, revealing that Elmquist's black hair was plastered wetly against his head.

"You were in the pool," Jupiter accused.

"I wasn't—" Elmquist began a denial, then felt a drop of water run down his face from his hair. "I was just in the shower," he said.

"No, you were just in the pool," corrected Jupe. "There are wet footprints leading to your door."

Elmquist looked down at the evidence and shrugged. "Okay, so I was in the pool. It was a rough day at the market, and a swim makes a guy relax. What of it?"

"Where's the Carpathian Hound?" cried

Prentice. "You scoundrel! You young thief!"

"I don't know what you're talking about!" said Elmquist. But his eyes darted sideways, towards his tiny kitchen.

"In one of the cupboards, I imagine," said Jupiter. "You haven't had time to hide it anywhere else."

"You're out of your mind!" protested Elmquist.

"Mr Prentice," said Jupiter, "I think you had better call the police. Tell them to come and bring a search warrant."

"You can't search this place!" cried Elmquist. "You can't get a warrant in the middle of the night!"

"Perhaps not," said Jupe. "Very well, we'll wait until morning and we'll get a search warrant then. In the meantime, we will be in the courtyard and you will not be able to leave your apartment without being seen."

"You can't do that!" Elmquist was almost shouting. "That's . . . that's harassment!"

"I don't see why," said Jupe. "There's no law against our sitting out in the courtyard, where we can't help seeing if you leave. But why make extra trouble for yourself? Give us the dog now and we won't have to ask the police to get it."

Elmquist glared at him for a few seconds, then stepped back out of the doorway.

"It's in the oven," he said. His voice was sullen. "I was going to give it back to you, Mr Prentice. Honest."

Fenton Prentice sniffed. "Were you going to

give it back after you got the ten thousand?"

"Ten thousand?" Sonny Elmquist looked truly bewildered. "What ten thousand?"

"You don't know?" said Jupiter Jones. "You really don't know about the money?"

Sonny Elmquist stared at them. "I thought Mr Prentice might want to give me a reward, for getting the dog back. But ten thousand dollars?"

Fenton Prentice stepped past Sonny Elmquist and walked to the kitchen. He opened the oven door. The crystal hound was there, the gilt string wrapped around it.

"Mr Prentice, I don't believe he does know about the money," said Jupiter. "He isn't the burglar. He's only a wanderer who happened to see something in his sleep."

Sonny Elmquist started and went several shades paler. His Adam's apple bobbed as he swallowed.

"What did you see, Elmquist?" demanded Jupe. "When you fall asleep here with the television on, what do you see?"

Elmquist was shaking now.

"I can't help it," he said. "I dream things. I can't help it, can I, if I dream things?"

"What did you dream?" Jupe persisted.

"I dreamed about a dog, a glass dog. I dreamed that someone came in the dark, late at night, and put the dog into the water. I couldn't see who it was."

"I think," said Jupiter to his friends, "that he's telling the truth."

18

The Booby-trapped Ransom

SONNY ELMQUIST's face looked pinched. "Look, you guys, I got the dog out of the pool for Mr Prentice. I was going to give it to him. Honest I was. And I didn't steal it in the first place."

"No," said Jupe, "you didn't. You were asleep when the burglary took place. But you did hide the crystal dog once you found it. That doesn't look very good."

Charles Niedland leaned against the wall. "Go and get some clothes on and come upstairs," he ordered. "We want you where we can keep an eye on you."

Elmquist glared at Niedland. "You have no right to order me around!" he yelled. "You don't own the building."

"And you have no right to invade my apartment, in whatever form," said Fenton Prentice. "You will do as you are told or I'll call the police and have you arrested for holding stolen property!"

Elmquist turned and slammed into his bedroom. The boys heard closet doors bang open and drawers being pulled out. In a few minutes Elmquist was back, dressed in a black sweater and light pants.

"You will spend the night in my living room, and you will *not* go to sleep," said Prentice.

Sonny Elmquist nodded sullenly.

Prentice cradled his crystal hound. "I suppose Jupiter, that you still wish to catch the burglar tonight?"

"If possible—if we haven't scared him off with our noise."

Prentice handed the dog over reluctantly, and he and Charles Niedland led Elmquist upstairs. The Investigators replaced the Hound in the pool and resumed their watch from the balcony.

If he had ever planned to retrieve the dog, the burglar did not do so that night. The long, cold, dark hours passed quietly, and at last the dawn came, grey and foggy.

"He wouldn't really have to get the dog out of the pool," said Jupe finally. "He'd simply have to collect the money from Mr Prentice and then let him know where the dog was."

The door behind the boys opened. "Breakfast?" inquired Fenton Prentice. He was dressed as immaculately as ever, and seemed greatly refreshed.

Everyone sat down to eat except Sonny Elmquist. He slouched on a chair in the den and refused either to eat or to talk.

After breakfast, Jupiter found a day-old newspaper and began cutting it into small rectangles— each one about two inches wide and five inches long.

"What are you doing that for?" Bob asked.

"Soon the burglar should tell us when to deliver the ransom. We should have a package of money ready for him," said Jupe. "Mr Prentice knows where his dog is, so he won't want to deliver real money."

"Why deliver anything?" asked Pete.

"Because we want proof of who the burglar is," said Jupiter. "We'll treat the package of money with my special ointment. We may not get to see the burglar claim the ransom. But if he picks up my package, he'll soon have indelible black spots on his hands. Then we'll have him!"

"You are assuming, of course, that we know him," said Fenton Prentice.

"Of course we know him," said Jupe happily. "He is aware of Gwen Chalmers' fondness for chocolates. He knows that Mrs Bortz does her shopping at four in the morning. He *must* be a tenant here."

"Hassell!" exclaimed Pete. "He's the only one left!"

Jupe smiled and said nothing.

"You know who it is!" said Prentice.

"I know, but I can't prove it," Jupe told him. "Not yet. When he tries to collect the ransom, *then* we'll have proof!"

Jupe would say no more. When the mail arrived at ten, he had two neat stacks of clipped newspaper piled on the living room table.

The postman left a letter in Fenton Prentice's mailbox—a typed, unsigned letter.

WRAP THE MONEY IN BROWN PAPER
AND LEAVE IT IN THE WASTE-PAPER
BASKET AT THE ENTRANCE TO THE
PARK AT EXACTLY FIVE THIS AFTER-
NOON.

The message was on a plain sheet of white bond,
and the postmark on the envelope was for the
previous day.

"Good!" said Jupe, smiling with satisfaction.
He proceeded to dab ointment on the exposed
newspaper dollars while Mr Prentice located some
brown paper. Then he wrapped the bogus ransom
and treated the outside of the package with more
ointment.

"There," he said to Mr Prentice. "At five,
simply walk down to the corner and put this
package into the waste-paper bin, as the burglar
directs. I suggest that you protect your hands
from the ointment by wearing old gloves. Of
course, you'll want to contact the police first.
They'll stake out the park, and when the burglar
picks up the package, they'll catch him."

"Suppose some tramp picks up the package,"
said Prentice. "There isn't any shortage of people
who go through rubbish bins."

"I don't think the burglar will let that happen,"
said Jupe. "He'll be watching."

"Aren't we going to be in at the finish?"
demanded Pete.

"Of course. At five, we'll be watching the
waste-paper bin, too. You won't see us, Mr
Prentice, but we'll be there!"

19

The Perfect Alibi

By 4.45, Bob, Pete, and Jupiter had concealed themselves in the shrubbery next to the parish house. The little park at the foot of the street was deserted except for a maintenance man, who wandered to and fro with a sack and a stick, spearing bits of rubbish out of the grass.

"The burglar will come from Wilshire," predicted Jupiter.

A newspaper van rolled down the street and pulled into the kerb near the entrance to the park. A man jumped down from the back, took out a stack of newspapers, and put them on the pavement. The van went on and the man stood by the papers as if waiting for customers to appear.

Behind the boys, a window opened in the rectory. "I think," said a familiar voice, "that you'll be more comfortable if you wait inside!"

Pete turned. Father McGovern stood in the open window smoking a pipe.

"It's not seemly to be skulking in the bushes," he said. "Come around to the front door and I'll let you in. You can watch everything from here."

Jupiter Jones felt his face get red.

"It's not invisible you are," said the pastor.

149

"Come in, now. The police will not want you tampering with their affairs again."

The boys got themselves quickly out of the shrubbery and into the parish house.

"I saw you come down the street," the priest told them. "Those men out there—the one with the newspapers and the one with the sack—they're waiting for someone. Has it to do with Earl and the robbery?"

"I think they're undercover men, Father," said Jupiter.

"I *know* one of them is," the priest told them. "The man with the sack is Sergeant Henderson. He's been to see Earl at the hospital I met him there. The other I don't know. But we don't usually have a news vendor outside the park."

"You'd make a pretty good detective, Father!" said Bob. "How is Earl?"

"He'll be all right. He was pleased, I think, to find out that someone probably struck him. He doesn't like to admit that he might fall." The pastor relit his pipe, which had gone out. "As for Mrs O'Reilly," he said, "it's her afternoon off, which is why I'm smoking in the parlour."

Jupiter Jones grinned, then looked at his watch. "Almost five," he announced.

Fenton Prentice came down the street carrying the brown paper parcel. He stopped at the path that led into the park. A waste-paper bin stood there, full almost to overflowing. Prentice looked around, then put the parcel into the bin and walked back up the street.

Immediately a man rounded the corner from Wilshire. He looked a complete derelict. The collar of his ragged coat was pulled up to hide the fact that he wore no shirt and the cuff of one trouser leg was torn.

"Ah, now!" said Father McGovern. "Poor soul!"

The tramp approached the entrance to the park. The maintenance man was several yards away, stooping to examine something he had found on the grass. The news vendor counted his papers.

The ragged man poked into the waste-paper bin. A second later the brown parcel was in his hands. Then it vanished, hidden under his coat.

The news vendor ran towards the tramp.

The maintenance man dropped his stick and his sack and ran, too.

The tramp saw the two men coming. He darted into the street. Pete threw open the parlour window and jumped out.

A horn blared, and a car swerved to avoid hitting the tramp. The tramp raced on.

As Pete ran forward, the policemen shouted. One fired his gun into the air. The tramp reached the corner of Wilshire, turned right, and disappeared.

"Excuse me, Father!" said Jupiter, and he went out the window, too, with Bob after him.

"Hey, you kids!" yelled the policeman who had been pretending to sell papers. "Out of the way." He motioned to Pete to stay back.

A squad car zoomed up the street and screeched to the kerb. "He headed west on Wilshire," cried

Sergeant Henderson, the maintenance man, to the officer in the car.

"Wait!" yelled Jupe.

The policemen glared at him. "What?" said one.

"No hurry," said Jupiter. "I know where the burglar is—and his package of bogus ransom. He won't try to hide. He's got a perfect alibi."

"Oh, you're the smart kid Mr Prentice talked about," said Sergeant Henderson. "Okay, kid, where is he?"

"He is, or in a few moments will be, at the Belvedere Medical Clinic," said Jupiter Jones. "It's only a few blocks from here."

The man at the wheel of the squad car scowled, then said, "Okay. Get in!"

The Three Investigators tumbled into the back seat. The car roared off and reached the clinic in no time. The pink-smocked receptionist was outraged when the Investigators and the policemen stormed past her desk without even consulting her.

On the second floor, a nurse was just coming on duty. She paused and stared at them.

"Whom do you wish to see?" she demanded. "The front desk didn't call me!"

"Never mind," said Jupiter. He was striding down the corridor to the big corner room occupied by John Murphy.

The door was closed. Jupe pushed it open and saw Murphy in bed, the covers pulled up to his chin. The television set on the wall opposite the bed was on. Murphy took his eyes from the TV and looked at the group in the doorway.

"What is it?" he asked.

"Is the package of money in the closet, Mr Murphy?" asked Jupiter. "Or did you hide it under the bedclothes?"

Murphy sat up. His face was flushed and his breathing was raspy. The bedcovers slipped down. He had on a tattered jacket and no shirt.

Jupiter opened the door of the closet. The wrapped parcel was there, still sealed.

Murphy groaned.

"Even if you'd gotten rid of it on the way back to the hospital, we'd still know," said Jupiter. "It was treated with special ointment, and your hands will shortly be covered with black spots.

Murphy looked down at his hands.

Sergeant Henderson stepped forward. "You have the right to remain silent," he told Murphy.

"Never mind," said the man in the bed. "I know my rights. I'll get my clothes on and I want to call my lawyer."

The sergeant stared at the Three Investigators. "Prentice said you were smart," he told them. "A perfect alibi. A private hospital. Who'd ever think . . . ?"

"Murphy set that fire in his apartment himself!" said Jupe. "He wanted an excuse to be in the hospital! He knew there wouldn't be many patients here between Christmas and New Year. He wasn't really hurt. Once he learned the nurses' routines, he could slip in and out. They weren't watching him that closely—they wanted him to get some sleep!"

20

A Visit to Mr Hitchcock

IT WAS mid-January before the Three Investigators were able to arrange an appointment with
Alfred Hitchcock. They found the famous motion-
picture director in his office, paging through a
copy of *Art News* magazine.

"If you are going to tell me the tale of the
Carpathian Hound," said Mr Hitchcock, "I can
save you the trouble. There is an illustrated
article on the work of the late Edward Niedland
in this publication. The crystal dog is shown, and
the old legend is recounted."

Mr Hitchcock put down the magazine. "However, if you have come to tell me how the stolen
Hound was restored to Fenton Prentice, I should
be delighted to hear the details. The accounts in
the newspapers were quite brief."

"Mr Prentice doesn't like publicity," said Bob.

"So I understand," said Mr Hitchcock. "However, he did mention that three lads from Rocky
Beach had been of great help to him, so I've been
expecting you. I assume that you have had time
to write up the case?"

Bob handed a file folder to the director. "Aha!"
said Mr Hitchcock.

As was his custom, he did not comment until he had read carefully through Bob's notes. When he finished, he closed the file and sat for a moment, frowning.

"Amazing!" he exclaimed at last. "And I am not easily amazed. A person who can go to sleep, depart from his material body, and allow his spirit to wander free! Elmquist makes the ordinary ghost seem almost a bore."

"He still hasn't admitted his special ability," said Bob. "As Professor Lantine said, many of the people who wander won't admit it. It scares them."

"Understandably!" said Mr Hitchcock. "Now, Jupiter, how did you know that Murphy had to be the burglar?"

"It was a simple process of elimination," said Jupe. "First I realized that the burglar had to be someone in the neighbourhood—someone who knew about the keys to the church in the parish house closet. When Miss Chalmers and Mrs Bortz were removed from the scene, I knew the burglar had to be a fellow tenant. Only a tenant would have the necessary knowledge of their habits—and only a tenant would know the swimming pool was a safe place once they were gone.

"Now, Sonny Elmquist was asleep when the burglary took place, so he couldn't be guilty. Bob's investigation at Ruxton confirmed that. Bob learned that Elmquist could possibly be in two places at once, but that he couldn't *do* anything, move anything, while he wandered. Harley Johnson had an easily checked alibi for the night of the burglary. That left Alex Hassell and John Murphy.

"Both Hassell and Murphy were away from home at the time of the burglary," continued Jupe. "And both heard Mrs Bortz announce that she was going to drain the pool. I remembered later that her words startled Murphy. And later that evening he drove off somewhere."

"No doubt to get the explosive," put in Mr Hitchcock. "It isn't the sort of thing one keeps around the house."

"He went to a friend who manufactures chemicals," said Jupe. "The device he wired to Mrs Bortz's car wasn't really deadly, but it did make a lot of noise and smoke. He only wanted to upset her so that she'd forget about the pool for a day or two. That's all the time he needed—a day or two.

"I would have been sure sooner that Murphy was the burglar if it hadn't been for that fire in his apartment. I didn't think it was an accident because Murphy *was* careful with his cigarettes. He looked like still one more victim of the criminal. He had no apparent connection with the pool, but I thought that possibly the burglar wanted to remove all potential witnesses. So I began to think that Alex Hassell was the criminal —that he had gotten into Murphy's apartment and set the fire in some way. We wouldn't have seen him—we weren't watching our TV monitor carefully when the fire started. Hassell could then have moved to the motel to try to establish an alibi, just as Murphy actually had himself moved to the hospital.

"But when the letter came with the directions for the delivery of the ransom, I knew the burglar couldn't be Hassell. It had to be Murphy. The ransom was to be put in the waste-paper bin in the park at exactly five o'clock, and that's when Hassell fed the cats! If Hassell had been the burglar, the ransom would have been delivered at some other time—never at five."

Mr Hitchcock laughed. "No. Never at five. Even if he had been willing to keep the cats waiting, he wouldn't have dared to say five o'clock. His absence would have been noticed. But why did Murphy take such chances for ten thousand dollars? He was a reputable broker. Did he need money that badly?"

"He thought he did," Jupe answered. "He confessed that, as Harley's guardian, he had borrowed money from Harley's account for his own speculations on the stock market. He lost it all. Harley will be of age next month. At that time, Murphy would have to explain the missing money—and the explanation would put him in jail. So he desperately needed ten thousand dollars to put back into Harley's account."

Mr Hitchcock sighed. "A sad story, and an old one."

"Harley has forgiven him," said Jupiter. "But of course, the matter is out of Harley's hands. It's up to the courts. Murphy did strike Earl, and he did send poisoned chocolates to Gwen Chalmers so that she'd be too ill to swim. And he did commit a burglary and attempt to extort money from Mr Prentice."

"Which brings us to another point," said Mr Hitchcock. "How did Murphy know the Carpathian Hound would be at Lucan Court that day?"

"Sonny Elmquist told him!" said Bob. "Jupe was right all along—there was a connection between the shadow in Prentice's apartment and the burglary. You see, last Monday Elmquist's astral body overheard Prentice on the phone, making arrangements with Charles Niedland for the delivery of the dog. At least, that's what we think happened. Elmquist denies it—claims he heard the story from Mrs Bortz earlier. But she didn't know exactly when the Hound was arriving.

"At any rate, after Elmquist woke up from his wandering, he ran into Murphy in the courtyard and mentioned the Hound to him. Elmquist didn't know what the Hound really was—but Murphy knew the name Niedland and could guess. So he went over to Lucan Court with a ski mask and gun, intending to hold up Niedland."

"He certainly *was* desperate," commented Mr Hitchcock.

"Yeah, and he got more so!" put in Pete. "I mean, he thought he could just grab the crystal dog and run right home. Everything looked a cinch when Niedland wasn't even there. But then the cops came and almost caught him. He didn't dare go home, so he ran into the church and started thinking fast. He posed as a statue, then beaned poor old Earl with his gun, and hid the crystal dog. Then he slipped outside, tossed his mask and dark jacket in the rubbish bin near the park, and strolled home."

"And went back for the dog the next night, disguised as the phantom priest!" exclaimed the director.

Jupe shook his head. "No. Murphy told us that *he* saw the phantom priest, too!"

"Hm!" said Alfred Hitchcock.

"It shook him up a lot," Pete continued. "But he pulled himself together and beat it, locking in Jupe behind him. Later, after everything quietened down, he lowered the dog into the pool. We figure Elmquist was wandering around in his astral body and saw him do it. Elmquist was home that night."

"What will happen to Elmquist?" asked the director.

"Nothing," said Pete. "Maybe he intended to commit a crime and hold on to the Hound, but he didn't actually do it. He didn't have a chance. He's still hoping to get to India, but right now he isn't going any farther than West Los Angeles. Mr Prentice got in touch with the company that owns the building. They made Elmquist move."

"Has his astral body returned to haunt Prentice?" Mr Hitchcock wanted to know.

"No. He's been gone two weeks now, and Mr Prentice has had nothing but peace. Mrs Bortz left, too. Said the neighbourhood was going to the dogs, with all those crimes, and she just couldn't be responsible. Mr Prentice has a new manager in the apartment house. He says she doesn't care what the tenants do, so long as they don't play their stereos too loud or swim after ten at night. Mr Prentice is very glad. He doesn't have to worry about snoopers any more."

"So all of his problems have been solved," said Mr Hitchcock. "But there is still the matter of the phantom priest."

"Possibly Elmquist in his astral body," said Jupiter. "When seen in his astral form, he was always wearing whatever his real body then wore. In a white turtleneck and dark sweater, he might look like a priest at a distance. But there's still the problem of the white hair—Elmquist's is black—and the candle. I don't think an astral body can hold a real, flickering candle.

"A second possibility is that the phantom priest was Elmquist in the flesh. Elmquist's astral body might have seen the crystal dog in the church, and Elmquist himself might have come over to investigate. Assuming he had a little larceny in his heart, he could have disguised himself as the phantom priest to scare off anyone who came in. But there's a problem with this explanation, too—how would Elmquist get outside again when the doors were locked after my rescue?"

Alfred Hitchcock nodded. "And that leaves you with a third possibility . . ."

"That there *is* a phantom priest!" finished Bob. "We will never really know."